TROUBLESHOOTER ON TRIAL

When it was known that Jock McArthur's kinsman was coming on a visit from Scotland, Mike Liddell took time off from his job as troubleshooter at the Beauclerc place and rode to meet him. Unfortunately, Quentin McArthur, a reckless Highland Scot, was killed by an unknown gun before he reached his destination. Mike found himself facing a possible hanging charge due to perjured evidence by Beauclerc enemies, and the Marden gang of reformed outlaws had to risk their own freedom to save him.

Books by David Bingley
in the Linford Western Library:

THE BEAUCLERC BRAND
ROGUES REMITTANCE
STOLEN STAR
BRIGAND'S BOUNTY

DAVID BINGLEY

TROUBLESHOOTER ON TRIAL

Complete and Unabridged

LINFORD
Leicester

First published in Great Britain in 1980

First Linford Edition
published 2003

British Library CIP Data

Bingley, David, *1920 –*
    Troubleshooter on trial.—Large print ed.—
    Linford western library
    1. Western stories
    2. Large type books
    I. Title
    823.9′14 [F]

    ISBN 0–7089–9461–X

Published by
F. A. Thorpe (Publishing)
Anstey, Leicestershire

Set by Words & Graphics Ltd.
Anstey, Leicestershire
Printed and bound in Great Britain by
T. J. International Ltd., Padstow, Cornwall

This book is printed on acid-free paper

1

The township of Sundown City in Sunset County, New Mexico territory, quaked in the heat of a mid-summer afternoon. Boards in the buildings on Main Street occasionally creaked as the sun poured down its power and rendered even drier, timbers which had seemingly given up all moisture.

Dogs cowered in the shade, their tongues lolling out pitifully. No one was abroad, other than those whose business was most pressing.

In the town marshal's office, two men had talked for nearly fifteen minutes. One of them was Abel Smith, the marshal, and the other — his visitor — was the town's celebrated Scottish blacksmith, old Jock McArthur.

Jock was a bulky, stooping, bald-headed character. As he talked, he toyed with his shapeless dun-coloured

1

stetson, his fingers working it as though it were clay. He wore his black leather working apron over his denims and shirt; he looked even hotter than the beads of perspiration on his brow suggested.

'All right, then, marshal,' the old Scot murmured. 'I'll no keep you any longer. You'll give young Liddell the gist of what I've said to you, an' pass my kind regards to the lady of the house, and her staff. *Adios*, Abel.'

'I will, I will,' the marshal assured him.

Smith had been dying to get rid of his loquacious visitor for quite a while, but he needed to stay on the right side of the old Scotsman, who had a lot of prestige in the town, including being on the visiting list of *Madame la Baronne de Beauclerc*, the titled French lady who owned the chateau to the north of the town.

Favouring his stiff leg, a relic of his cattle-droving days, the poker-faced peace officer hopped out onto the sidewalk after his visitor, who was stepping out briskly and slapping his apron with the calloused fingers of his left hand.

'You'll need to take a siesta, Jock, if trade is slack!'

The Scotsman nodded and glanced back over his shoulder. 'I'd have been up to the chateau meself, only I thought maybe they'd think I was toutin' for business.'

As the distance between them lengthened both characters laughed. The broiling heat made Smith blow air from his mouth into his stiff, greying handlebar moustache. For two or three days he had wanted to visit the chateau, and yet he had not felt — until Jock's visit — that he had reasonable grounds for making the trip.

Skipping adroitly indoors, the marshal crossed the scarred floor using a unique pivoting gait which he favoured when no one was around to see him. He grabbed a big bunch of keys from his desk, crossed to the door which led to the cell block, and gave himself access to the first cell.

At that time, the town had only one important villain under lock and key, and he had been placed in a more substantial building, wide of town, with a constable and a deputy marshal in fairly close attendance throughout the day and night.

Having the peace office to himself suited the marshal. Inside the first cell, he had a large wall mirror, a metal wash basin, which he kept filled with cool water, a cut-throat razor, a brush and comb and one or two other items which he used for his personal grooming.

He worked on the moustache first, thinning it and trimming its extremities. He glared at his image, giving it the flinty-eyed look in the mirror, thinking over the startling events of a few weeks back, and wondering if the trouble connected with the attempted kidnapping of *Madame la Baronne* was truly over.

Fifteen minutes later, Smith was

ready for the visit. In the old days, when there had been little communication between the chateau and its private guards and the rest of the town, Smith would have run out his horse in order to cut a better figure, and to hide his game leg for as long as possible.

Now, he felt he had to add prestige to his office by appearing as fit as possible. In his well-brushed dark suit and black low-crowned hat, he set off on the long walk. He soon felt glad that there were few townspeople about, and there was a certain relief when he changed direction for the north and achieved some shade.

The Chateau Beauclerc looked pretty, desirable and vulnerable to his practised lawman's eye. There was no one in sight on the garden side of the east-west white-painted low fences, nor beyond the trimmed hedges which masked the southern end of the main frontage, back from the north-south avenue of trees.

And yet he knew that watchful eyes

were not far away. The shutters were drawn on the floors above the main entrance, on account of the heat. The beautiful residence had a somnolent look about it.

Perspiration was beading his brow, and sticking his clean shirt to his body. A slight feeling of inferiority made him hurry past the front door and hastily turn the corner between the house and the nearest outbuilding, a stable.

At once he became aware of voices in the back garden. In fact, it sounded almost like a garden party. The rather distinctive but charming Irish accent of Molly O'Callan, *la Baronne*'s housekeeper, came through and was followed by a chuckle. The chuckle sound was swallowed up in a high-pitched trill of laughter which could only have been made by the teenage Mexican housemaid, Carmelita.

A man's baritone voice joined in the merriment, but his contribution was short-lived. Someone had detected the sound of approaching footsteps.

Suddenly, everything beyond the skirting hedge went quiet. There was a rustling and a sudden thud, as if some item of furniture had been overturned. Finally, the unmistakable click of a six-gun hammer.

Although he could see no one, Smith felt isolated, and observed by many pairs of eyes. Where he had perspired before, the moisture now came out of him as though his pores had suddenly become enlarged. His right hand strained against his better judgement to go closer to the holster by his right thigh. He withstood the pressing inclination and cleared his throat rather noisily.

'Who's callin'?' the baritone voice queried.

It came from several feet away from where the gun had clicked.

'Abel Smith, the marshal. On a social call. Sorry if I disturbed you.'

His voice revealed the dryness of his throat, and the strain which had been caused by the sudden tension beyond the fence.

The same voice said: 'Come on through, marshal. Sorry if we over-reacted. The time was when you could have wandered all the way over the property without bein' disturbed. But it ain't so any more, and you know why.'

Chuckling mirthlessly, Marshal Smith moved forward about five yards from the side of the shed, and negotiated the gap in the thick green hedge. As he did so, those who had been relaxing on the back lawn stood up and looked a trifle sheepish.

Mike Liddell, Madame's official troubleshooter in times of strife, spun a forty-five Colt by the trigger guard, pointed it towards the ground and casually dropped it on the grass beside his gun belt. Mike was a tall, sinewy Texan, with hair like ripe corn and intense blue eyes. On this occasion he was wearing only a cream stetson, denim levis and a pair of moccasins. The toe had been cut out of one moccasin to accommodate a damaged big toe, still enlarged by a white bandage.

Molly O'Callan's green eyes were now mirroring mischief instead of apprehension. Carmelita, the plump Mexican girl, rose from her knees and put the sturdy wooden kitchen chair back on its four feet again.

Molly was wearing a white barber's cloth around her shoulders like a towel or shawl. She saw the funny side of her appearance, as the girl licked her lips and began to click the hair-cutting scissors in her restless fingers.

Short snippets of fine copper-coloured hair confirmed that it was Molly who had been having her hair cut when the unexpected visitor intruded.

'Seems like I'm jest in time for a hair cut,' Smith remarked. 'Can I ask whose turn is next?'

The tension finally dispersed. Mike Liddell gestured for the newcomer to take a chair, or squat on the grass, while Molly resumed her place on the barber's chair and made a remark about sweeping up the clippings to stuff a pillow or something. For a time, Carmelita's youthful bosom shook with laughter and her long, centrally-parted dark hair got in the way of her hair dressing.

Mike spun his stetson on an index finger. 'So, we're right in thinkin' you're not here to break bad news, Abel? I mean, the town hasn't lost that villain who ramrodded *Madame's* kidnap. Or anything?'

'Nope. Nothin' at all like that, Mike. I do have some information, regardin' kin of Jock McArthur, an' another fellow. Chap with an Irish background. Only information, you understand. May not be of interest to anyone here.'

The young Texan nodded. He then made a gesture towards the remotest part of the garden. Marshal Smith followed the apparent direction, and he was just in time to catch sight of a bleak, leathery face topped by a Quaker-style hat disappear from view behind yet another trimmed hedge.

10

Muted voices carried from the remote patch. Clearly, there were three men and they had also been alerted when the marshal showed up. He knew who they were. They were Earl Martin and his two assistants: the proprietor and work team of the Sunset Undertaking Agency. These three had been actively involved with Mike Liddell in safe-guarding Beauclerc life and property on more than one occasion. Right at that moment, they were supposed to be doing some repairs to a tunnel entrance which led into the house through the garden.

Molly called to the kitchen. 'You there, Joseph? Bring out some of that beer in the clay jug which came from the Sundowner! An' bring plenty of glasses!'

The high-pitched gentle voice of Joseph, Madame's elderly negro butler, answered. 'I hear you, Miss Molly. I'll be right out there!'

Two minutes later, the old man appeared, his seamed face brightened by a wide cheerful grin. His short-cropped silver hair caught the sunlight as he poured out the beer. Molly and Carmelita chatted, and the three men drew closer together.

'So tell us the news, marshal,' Mike prompted gently.

Smith removed froth from his imposing moustache with a thumb and forefinger. 'Well, you remember you were sayin' *Madame la Baronne* had given permission for some friends to make the journey out to Sunset, to come a-visitin'?'

Mike nodded, handed him a short cigar and lighted it for him.

'Seems like the relation of our blacksmith has made it as far as Pecos Town. Over to the south-west.'

The audience missed nothing. The young Texan pushed back his hat and drew on his own cigar, patiently awaiting other revelations. Pecos Town had scarcely been on the map when Mike Liddell first came into Sunset County. There was a town on Pecos

Creek which used 'Pecos Creek' as its name, but Pecos Town had literally sprung up in a matter of weeks because of the activities of a squad of telegraph line workers pushing communications towards the river Pecos and places further west.

Mike studied the burning butt of his cigar. 'I would have thought he'd arrive in these parts from the east coast, or the Gulf of Mexico. After all, Scotland, although it's a great distance away, is to be found in that direction.'

The marshal shrugged.

'Geography never was a strong point with me, Marshal,' Smith protested. 'I only know what Jock told me. He said his kin, a cousin or a nephew, was a wild fellow from the highlands of Scotland. Some well meanin' guy had brought word from Pecos Town that one Quentin McArthur was makin' a name for himself in the new town, as well as helpin' to extend the line of poles for the telegraph wire.'

Mike Liddell rolled on the grass and

propped his head on an elbow. The crowsfeet wrinkles at the corners of his eyes were well marked as he squinted across at the visitor.

'What Jock is sayin' is that his cousin is sailin' a bit close to the wind. Might get himself put in a western jail for something that would be hushed up in his own country. Now, what about the other fellow? The one you said was Irish?'

At the mention of the Irishman, Molly O'Callan tensed up. She brushed aside the scissors with which Carmelita was putting the finishing touches to her hair cut, but allowed the girl to brush out her shortened, wavy hair. Clearly, Molly wanted to hear every word spoken about the man from Ireland.

'Youngish man, name of Paddy McAllen. The name sounds quite a bit like that of Molly, only Jock thought it was spelled different.'

Slowly and painstakingly, Abel Smith explained the spelling difference between McAllen, and O'Callan. Mike thought he was labouring the point a bit, possibly with the intention of making Molly feel less concerned. The explanation did not seem to do anything for the shapely housekeeper.

Mike sniffed. 'If the name was definitely different, why does Jock think there's a connection with the chateau?'

After blowing cigar smoke down his nostrils, Smith talked with it dribbling from his mouth. 'Because when he was in liquor he talked of a big house, the property of a French family, an' the female kin who worked there, an' the sort of life he was goin' to live, after he'd made contact.'

Having made his explanation, Marshal Smith expected to be inundated with questions, but no one had anything further to say. His words seemed to hang on the air in the flower-perfumed garden. The peace officer felt out of his depth again. The cordiality was still there, but it seemed more formal. Ten minutes later, he talked of returning to his office.

He was thanked, but not pressed to stay. As soon as he was on his way, the small impromptu party in the garden broke up. Mike was left with Molly, who strolled up the lawn with him.

She murmured: 'I haven't seen him for sixteen years, since the three of us came off the boat, Mike. It'll be him, all right. He strikes fear into me. He's a bad lot.'

Molly never overreacted, and Mike believed her. Later, in the cool of the evening, he strolled in the garden with the tall, shapely, aristocratic blonde lady owner of the house. Madeleine, *la Baronne de Beauclerc*, was still in a nervous state following her abortive kidnap and a violent attack upon her home in her absence. But she listened well, cloaked in an expensive blue poncho and with her magnificent head of blonde hair hidden in a silk square of the same colour.

From time to time, she glanced at Michael, as he talked. She was weighing up his physical condition, as well as his words.

For the first time, his damaged toe was hidden in a riding boot. Against his inclinations, she had insisted upon a local boot-maker designing a special pair, to give him extra room over the toe.

After a time, *la Baronne* seated herself on a bench and beckoned for Michael to join her. 'All right, then. Our friend, Jock, thinks his relation might want some sort of protection on the way here from the new town, and Molly has fears about this wild cousin of hers.

'You've thought about it, and you feel you ought to ride over to Pecos Town and find out exactly what is going on in regard to the McArthur person and Molly's cousin. Is that right?'

Mike, looking well turned out in a blue shirt and new denims, nodded his agreement and awaited his employer's findings.

Madeleine rolled back the poncho

and took his hand. 'Michael, I don't need to conceal my feelings from you. You know how vulnerable I am. Will we be safe, if you go away? What about the chateau? And when is the trial of Charles Guérin to take place?'

'Earl Martin and his boys will remain here to guard you, indefinitely. Have no fears on that score. As for the trial of your kidnapper, that's to take place at Sunrise. It'll be the first big trial in the new county seat. But not for a month. Workers are putting the finishing touches to the county offices and court. So I'll be back in good time to escort you to Sunrise. That, I promise you.'

La Baronne smiled and shivered. Michael preceded her into the house to pour her a glass of cognac.

The following morning, he left town at daybreak, riding west.

2

The area immediately west of the mushrooming community known as Pecos Town was bad for crops and seemed to be constantly swept with hot dust, also on its way towards the meandering Pecos river. Apart from what shelter could be erected by the toiling telegraph gang of pole erectors, there was little in the way of foliage to alleviate the suffering of the perspiring team of mixed nationalities.

Inevitably, there were incidents. The heat combined with the interminable dust took a toll of men's tempers and made small happenings seem like heaven-sent build-ups to blood lettings.

Every evening, men made shelters out of the stacked poles which had arrived earlier in the day by freight wagons. Every morning, the temporary erections were left behind and the sun blazed down upon them once again. Sandy soil often penetrated the water wagon, and that affected the nerves of the steadiest.

The khaki tent of the manager, Gunther Prusse, flapped at times like the sails of a ship on the rocks. So much so that Prusse had two personal guards on the outside of his 'office' with strict orders to make sure that the tent did not blow away, as well as acting as armed guards when muscular pro-testers came hurrying towards the Boss's office.

At ten a.m. on the same day that Abel Smith took his information along to the Chateau Beauclerc, Heinz Kauffman, a stocky forty-year old American of German extraction, stag-gered along to the official tent with his small beady eyes red-rimmed with the dust.

Prusse's negro guard called: 'It's Heinz, the foreman, Boss. He's alone!'

'So send him in! Come on in, Heinz! What's keepin' you?'

Prusse was a tall man, three inches over six feet. Although he was nearing fifty years of age, his frame was still sparely covered with flesh. He had a small mouth, thin lips and a long, imposing Syrian nose which dominated his features. His dark hair was trimmed quite short under the brown derby hat which seldom left his head. His forehead was deeply lined. His eyes were heavily-lidded and hollowed.

When the negro called the warning, he had been on the point of removing a bottle from the smaller of two wooden chests, which comprised most of his office furniture. He hastily put the bottle back, closed the lid, and went through a nervous routine to make sure he was ready for his visitor. He was checking his weapons.

The Colt at his right hip was rigged for a left-handed cross draw. Most westerners, seeing the back-to-front holster for the first time, thought it quaint like the European riding breeches and the leather-patched work jacket. Few of them were ever wised up to the fact that Prusse's right arm was shorter than the other, on account of a duelling wound acquired twenty years earlier in Germany. Nor did they find out that Prusse carried a Derringer hideout gun and also a useful knife which was usually hidden by his jacket.

Kauffman undid the flap of the tent and stepped inside. He blinked a few times and mopped his eyes, while Prusse closed an account book and pushed aside the other papers which were strewn across his desk.

'Something wrong, Heinz?'

'Nothing that can't be put right, I guess, Boss. I'm annoyed, mostly. With one of the newcomers. That big Scot. Fellow with a peculiar name. Quentin. Quentin McArthur. The Irishman calls him Tammy. Something to do with the funny hat he wears. Sort of broad bonnet.'

Prusse, whose personal and private thirst was bugging him, cleared his throat. 'You want to sit down an' tell me all about it, Heinz?'

In contrast to Prusse, who was descended from military stock, Kauffman showed an entirely different attitude to life. He was of German farming stock, having come over to follow the soil, only to give it up due to his own restlessness and wayward ways. Just over average height, he was heavily muscled above the waistline, and also carrying an extra twenty pounds of flesh he did not need. His denim peaked cap added a bit of dignity to a face which had been flattened in the years immediately following his farming days. He had not earned much as a pugilist, but he did have one cauliflower ear.

Kauffman stopped leaning against one of the stout supporting poles and planted his broad posterior on the only other chair, which creaked.

'Now, what about the Scotsman?'

Kauffman shrugged his fleshy shoulders. 'Two days he worked like he knew his end was near. Now, he spoils it all.

Somebody must 'ave slipped him a bottle of fire water, or something. Shucks, Boss. I don't mind admittin' it, I don't understand these foreigners!'

Prusse opened and closed his heavy-lidded eyes a couple of times. He decided he did not have the patience to wait for a drink until his foreman had left, so he turned aside and produced the bottle of vodka again, and two glasses. Kauffman's red eyes appeared to improve as the drinks were poured out.

He was prompted again, as he received his glass.

'What did he do? Why, he scattered all the poles the other jaspers had set up ready to be dug in! Sort of grabbed them by the base, an' set them against his shoulder. Then he went off in a staggerin' run, an' heaved up on the bottom end!'

Prusse licked vodka off his thin lips. 'The poles did damage?'

'Not a lot,' Kauffman admitted grudgingly. 'Only he got more an' more ambitious, tossin' 'em further every time! He's got enough energy for ten men!'

The two in the tent did not realise how loudly the foreman had been talking until the negro backed up the lighter voice of the other guard, a pig-tailed Indian who did most of his communicating within himself.

Prusse pointed a sharp finger at Kauffman, and called: 'How's that again?'

'The Irishman, Boss. McAllen. Wants to talk to Kauffman, and possibly to both of you.'

A short pause engulfed the remote tent, its occupants and the trio outside.

'Shucks, like the man said, I only want to talk, gents! I got the best interests of the company at heart, I can assure you!'

Manager and foreman exchanged significant glances. The empty glasses were stowed away before the Irishman was permitted to enter.

Paddy McAllen grinned fitfully, first

at the foreman and then at the manager. 'Didn't want to interrupt nothing gents. Only wanted to say my buddy, McArthur, has calmed down. Stopped tossin' the cabers, as he calls it. In fact, he's sleepin'. I wanted to ask you to give him another chance. After all, he *is* a great worker, by any standards. Only, somebody produced an old newspaper, and Quentin figured this for a special day in the old country. That was all. Something to do with a great victory over the English, I suppose.

'Anyways, like I said, he's sleepin' it off, an' me, I'll make it my business to collect up the poles he's scattered, an' also to put the men back in a good humour.'

Prusse, who wanted another drink as soon as he was alone, made up his mind quickly. 'If you do as you've just suggested, and you guarantee to keep an eye on him, we'll overlook this foolish caper, just this once.'

McAllen knew not to overstay his

welcome. He said his thanks effusively and backed out, putting ground between him and the tent without looking back. Prusse and Kauffman watched him through the flap before the latter dogged the Irishman's footsteps back to the scene of action.

There was something about the Irishman's smile, his accent, his protruding ears and close-set eyes which marked him as different from the common run of railroad and telegraph labourers. Maybe it had something to do with the travel tales he told, or the way he tinkered around with his revolver, his knife and the set of throwing darts. However, he worked well at the critical times when the management was looking, and that counted for a lot.

McAllen strode on purposefully, passing the toiling men on the temporary platform, hitting in the umpteenth telegraph pole with a huge pair of hammers. The sweating, bearded twin operators, swinging alternately at the top of the pole, checked on their timing to glare at the Irishman, thinking that he had brought up some sort of ruse for missing out on work in the heat of the day.

McAllen jauntily touched his hat to them, and strolled on in the direction of those who were dragging poles along by mule power. The under foreman shouted a hoarse rebuke, but the Irishman waved his hand and called back that he had special orders from the manager.

Men who had been in the act of collecting up the scattered poles backed off as the newcomer purposefully walked his pinto pony into their midst and took the lariat off his saddle horn.

At one time, he had been pretty slick in the various skills of a cowpuncher, but a year or two had elapsed since he had done the punishing work. No less than a dozen labourers, stripped to the waist and partially protected by sweat rags at the throat and broad-brimmed hats, watched Paddy start up the new routine. He had to dismount to slip his loop under the end of the first one. In that, he reckoned, he lost face a little, but he managed to haul the pole away and dump it on a new heap some two hundred yards away.

The under foreman allowed the men to loaf around for the time it took, as he felt like a spell off himself. Then, the return of Kauffman changed things. Kauffman yelled and the other fellow added a hoarse cry. The labourers resumed, and McAllen went on with his work unimpeded and only casually observed.

By the time he had toted three of the timbers along, his body was dehydrating and he took no pleasure out of showing off in front of the other workers, most of whom cut a poor figure on a horse's back.

In order to distract himself from the worst rigours of the self-imposed task, he turned his inner thoughts to Quentin McArthur, and the remarkable revelations he had made when under the influence of malt whisky.

All that talk about coming thousands of miles to see his kin, one Jock McArthur, in the town of Sundown City. Jock being the town's main blacksmith. All that was of interest, but it was the talk about the huge French residence, owned by a titled French lady, name of Beauclerc, who had money to burn and servants galore, including a certain woman with beautiful deep auburn tresses with the unusual Irish name of O'Callan. That had turned him on.

O'Callan! Molly O'Callan, the second of the two female cousins who had come across from the Emerald Isle with him all those sixteen years ago.

Having dismounted and looped yet another pole, McAllen straightened up, using the pinto for temporary shade.

On the way across the Atlantic, on the boat, Molly and the other girl, name of Sheilagh, had taken a dislike to him. By a trick, the two women had given him the slip way back in Philadelphia.

For over fifteen years he had been out of touch with them. And now, his luck had changed!

He had actually been on his way to renew acquaintance with Sheilagh, who had married a dirt farmer and buried herself in a county of Arizona, when chance had caused the paths of McArthur and himself to cross. Molly was the one he would have gambled on to do well for herself. He had traced her years back to a town in Texas, but only after the family who employed her had pulled up their roots and dispensed with her services.

Although his mouth and throat were dry, he grinned.

Molly O'Callan, the housekeeper for the richest woman in the county. An aristocrat who could afford to send a Scotsman his travelling money to come from abroad, on account of a nodding acquaintance with an old blacksmith.

His confidence was high. He felt that at last he was about to strike it rich! No more doing the dirty work for Irish workers in the mines and furnaces, and falling foul of Pinkerton detectives. No more assassin jobs, and no more bounty hunting and having to keep on the move to avoid vengeance threats.

Molly O'Callan was going to make life easy for him in the near future. Either that, or he would spoil things for her in her snug little pampered nest!

He finished off his work with a wolfish grin on his dirt-streaked face and an old Irish melody on his dry lips.

3

That same afternoon a gaudily painted salesman's wagon was parked on an open lot at the rear of the Telegraph Hotel in the new settlement known as Pecos Town in the west of the county. The Hotel itself was a wooden hut with a sawdust floor, nothing more, but it had served as a saloon for a score of enterprising men whose compulsive need to make money was making a township out of nothing.

On the side of the wagon, the title *Waldo's Wagon* had been altered with a paint brush to read *Wally's Wagon*. Waldo was the previous owner. Given that the false-fronted Telegraph Hotel was overloaded, the current owner Wally Higgs, and his older sidekick, Rufe Simmons, were stretched out underneath the wagon, taking what ease was available to them in the oppressive heat.

Higgs was a pale, cunning young man of twenty-eight years. His nostrils had a permanent twitch. The wearing of black was habitual with him. A black stetson, jacket and trousers to match. His twin guns tended to swing a little on the low side, on account of his hips being exceptionally slim. On this occasion, he was lying chest downwards, hat pushed back, waistcoat unbuttoned and playing a solo game of cards with his half closed eyes too close to the paste boards for comfort.

'Rufe, when you allowed me to have my name on this wagon like I was the right an' proper owner, it felt good for a while. But now, well, I ain't so keen. Bein' a salesman ain't as fulfillin' as salivatin' someone for a proper fee.'

Rufe Simmons was a cylindrical, hirsute man in his early forties, quite weighty for his size. He could look quite friendly, amiable even, on occasion, on account of his round, toothy face and brown-haired, tonsured head. At that moment, he was leaking perspiration through his striped shirt and his expensive waistcoat, too. His balding head was resting upon the top of his flat, stiff-brimmed hat. He was unnecessarily manicuring his nails with his favourite weapon, a throwing knife.

'Aw, shut up, Wally! You're nothin' more than a spoiled kid! If I'd known the way you were goin' to turn out I'd never have married your mother, an' that's for sure! Never satisfied for more than a day or two. I don't know how to make you grow up, otherwise I'd fix it for you. Times are when I could carve your cards to pieces with this knife, an' nick little pieces out of you to teach you a lesson!'

The ill-assorted, lethal pair often quarrelled, but the lack of space and the heat were against any sort of physical brawl at that time.

Simmons groaned. 'The way I fixed old Waldo with one expert throw of my knife . . . when the wagon an' mules were crossin' that creek. Put my good name on the line, I did, an' you don't appreciate it, so help me!'

'I'm sorry, Rufe. Don't know how you've got the patience to put up with me. But I ain't felt so good since that dude troubleshooter belongin' to the French chateau got the better of us on the train. A man who lives by his weapons don't like to think there's a better stalkin' around the county not too far away. Besides, he could swear out a warrant for us, I guess . . . '

Simmons appeared not to have heard. 'You know how many dollars we turned over in one visit to the wire riggers' camp, Wally?'

Higgs nodded, and banged the back of his head on the timbers above him. 'Yer, yer, I know what you're gettin' at, Rufe. You an' me, we jest glimpsed a silver linin', didn't we?'

'*Four hundred an' thirty dollars, Wally, no less!*'

'I know, I know, an' we'll make more, before that there Melindy-Lou orders us into the firin' line again! She's a woman of spirit, that Melindy-Lou is! But tell me, Rufe, now you've had time to think over what we heard between that Scot an' the Irishman the other night . . .

'Do you think Melindy-Lou will make a strike against the Chateau Beauclerc, itself? Especially after what happened to the French officer, Guerin, an' that tough gang that got itself wiped out durin' the kidnap!'

Simmons stopped pairing his nails, turned ever so slightly, and began to do delicate things with the sharp tip of his blade. He tapped two or three cards with just sufficient force to make them jump on the sparse grass. And then he tapped it on the brim of Higgs' hat.

'Your voice ain't all that sweet, amigo! It carries. You could be tellin' someone who could profit by knowin' our true profession an' who our friends an' enemies are!'

Higgs recoiled and rolled to the edge, peering around to see if anyone was in a position to overhear. Simmons' telling words had some effect upon himself. He, too, did some wriggling and peered around in another direction. Higgs shook his head, and Rufe shrugged.

'I guess Melindy-Lou will already know more than the McArthur fellow, but we might be able to make use of him, sooner or later. One thing I *do* know, if McArthur the blacksmith is in cahoots with *La Baronne* an' that Mike Liddell, he ain't likely to become a close friend of mine.'

'All right, all right. Don't let's argue any more, Rufe. For me, Pecos Town ain't much more attractive than the end of wire. Why don't we make another trip out to the camp? If we don't like it we can always think of something else.'

'There's one thing you've overlooked, bein' a new businessman.'

'Explain to me, Rufe.'

'Sure. It's a matter of stock. In taking hundreds of dollars we depleted our stock. We need more, before we go out into the wilds again. Not bein' honest, we have to get replenished without payin' for it. Think you could break into that stock room, backin' onto the shack next door to the saloon? Without noise?'

Higgs chuckled. His laughter was high-pitched, the type which made people look round and take a second, closer look. The sound of it never grew commonplace to Simmons, but he was used to it.

Presently, they stepped clear of their resting place and briefly scouted the immediate area. All was quiet. Simmons attended to the lock of the rear door with his knife. Inside the stock room, Higgs started to chuckle again, but this time Simmons effectively stopped him with a painful kick on the shin.

After that, for ten minutes, the two thieves walked from the store to the wagon carrying boxes, small bales and bottles. Tobacco, liquor, cigars, snuff and canned food changed hands, until the wagon timbers started to protest.

It was then that Higgs noticed an

urchin of about ten years, furtively watching their antics from the other end of the alley between the saloon and the store. With his lips scarcely moving, he made known his findings to his partner. They made another trip each, before Simmons broke routine and waved to the boy, clearly inviting him closer. The lad wavered and then took to his heels. The thieves gradually relaxed. The actual stacking of the fresh goods in the wagon took them fifteen minutes.

At the end of that time, Simmons was as anxious to move as Higgs, but the urchin had turned up again, this time peering round the corner from the alley further along.

'Hey, son, you want something sweet to eat?' Simmons asked.

The lad shook his head. Simmons moved a little closer. 'Why are you so curious? Think we ought to turn out a tired store-keeper in the heat of the day?'

No reaction. Simmons gestured for

Higgs to go off by the nearer alley, so as to get behind the observer and cut off his retreat. Suddenly, the lad panicked. Simmons reacted, slipped his throwing knife down his sleeve and into his hand. He threw it with scarcely a second of hesitation. His aim was good. Had the lad not crouched a little, he might have been dead. As it was, he left his battered straw hat pinned to the fence.

And then he was gone. Simmons was marvelling that all this could go on in broad daylight without anyone being the wiser. Higgs could move with speed when he wanted to. He was slow to return, however, and gradually Simmons began to have doubts about the lad being cut off.

Presently, Wally returned, exaggerating his breathlessness.

'Somebody had started to build a sidewalk of sorts. He — must have crawled under it, or something. I never saw him go. So what do we do?'

Oddly enough, the rotund man showed no special reaction. He fetched the mules from the sparse plot where they had been resting, harnessed them to the wagon, mounted up and looked for Higgs to join him. Pecos Town was built on a slope. Simmons chose a downgrade and soon they were following other ruts made by vehicles.

'You ain't leavin' town, Rufe?'

The reply was a mere shrug of the thick shoulders.

'What do we say, if anyone challenges us?'

'If anyone challenges us, we rush forward with the dinero to pay the owner. Tell him his back entrance was standin' open an' we didn't want to disturb him. An' we knew he'd understand, an' we give a few things away, presents off the wagon. There's always a way, amigo. For a galoot with brains.'

The creek was narrow and far from clear, but the stunted trees which took their water from it provided shade of a sort.

As they dismounted and looked for a

more suitable resting place, Wally Higgs set his thin lips in a hard line, and shook his head.

'You'd be actin' out of character, handin' over bundles of notes for the stores we stole. There's something wrong about it all.'

Higgs tutted until Simmons' patience was exhausted. 'Aw, shucks, Wally. I didn't say the other fellow would be allowed to keep all the dinero, did I? You know me better than that. If I part with it, I'll get it back. Or more of the same sort.'

And with that, they settled to a temporary truce.

★   ★   ★

When Mike Liddell's chestnut horse plodded into Pecos Town a few hours later, there was still too much westering sun to allow for the lighting of lamps in the streets, but the heat had long since past its punishing worst and there were sights and sounds, people shouting, occasional laughter, and honkie-tonk music played with the loud pedal in full use.

The dollar extractors who always followed men doing hard physical work were trying to promote the conditions for reasonable business.

However, the serious-looking young Texan's mind was taken up with what Abel Smith had said about McArthur and McAllen. Mike found himself comparing what few facts he knew about Quentin McArthur from the highlands of Scotland with Paddy McAllen from that other piece of territory, Ireland.

A faint west-to-east breeze blew a mixture of desirable and undesirable smells into the face of the newcomer. The batwings of a saloon opened and closed as an early evening drinker sauntered out, studied the atmosphere and strolled back in again.

Distantly, the rider noticed the swinging sign which indicated the whereabouts of the peace office. He supposed that was where he ought to start looking, if he were to tidy up his worst fears — or confirm them.

An elderly constable with a sprouting grey moustache stopped his rocker on the sidewalk as the big fair, dusty rider dismounted by the hitchrail and nudged the sweating chestnut in the direction of a nearby water trough.

''Evenin' stranger. Hope you don't need a whole lot of help, 'cause the marshal is out visitin' an' the deputy is on what you might call continuous patrol. That leaves me, an' I'm better at jest lookin' rather than chasin' up villains.'

Mike chuckled, and pushed back his flat-crowned cream-coloured stetson. The constable did the same, but his stetson was perhaps ten years old and had been gradually darkening through most of that time. It had started out with a straight brim which now had ripples in it.

'Evenin', constable, I've just ridden over from Sundown, as a matter of fact.

45

Had word that a Scottish fellow, new to the district was tryin' to make a name for himself. Kind of loud, an' noisy, so his kin was told. You wouldn't know if anyone is on a charge, or merely sleepin' off the town's good liquor in the cells, would you?'

'Rest your mind on that, stranger. Ain't nobody occupyin' the cells right now. Don't go for it where it can be avoided. They tend to make the accommodation dirty, an' I happen to be the hombre who does the swabbin' out!'

The constable dissolved into laughter at his own droll way of putting things. Mike's shaking shoulders added to his pleasure.

'You don't happen to know a place where I can get a wash, a meal an' maybe a bed for the night, do you?'

'Ain't much scope, but you'd do all right with Big Annie. Annie Skinner, that is. Came along the telegraph line lookin' for a fellow, but he'd lit out afore she got here, so she's drummin' a livin' in a shack over the north side of Main. You'll see it. Plenty of washin' out down the back and down the side.'

Mike thanked him and started to ask about a livery, but the chair had started swinging again. The constable stuck up four fingers and a thumb, pointed towards the west end and then indicated right. The stable was, in fact, about fifty yards along. Having seen to the chestnut's needs, Mike tramped along to Big Annie's, and she sent him out at the back where he found a big tin tub. She filled it and insisted that he should use it, although she was already very busy dishing up the evening meal for about half a dozen hungry men.

Washed, changed and sated with beef, vegetables and fruit pie, Mike smoked a cigar on the shaded side of the building.

The hooting, yipping and firing off of six-shooters started around nine in the evening. Big Annie stuck her ample bosom out of the open window behind

47

the smokers, and selected Mike to be the recipient of information because he was the latest comer and he seemed to be the most interested.

Her voice was deep for a woman's, and her bulk made her seem taller than her five-and-a-half feet.

'You look surprised, mister,' she called to him. 'In these parts when the white man wants to play he acts like a Red Indian. Them whoopin' jaspers ridin' round the town on borrowed horses is off duty telegraph pole erectors from the gang workin' out at the end of the wire.

'On pay night they shoot up a few lamps, jest for devilment, but the peace officers don't often slap 'em in cells, 'cause they're a source of revenue to the likes of me.'

Two other smokers with their hats pushed forward would clearly have liked to inform Mike of Big Annie's special interest in the line workers, but she stayed where she was, effectively blocking the window and denying any of her lodgers the right to gossip in her presence.

Shortly after Annie had withdrawn to tackle her outstanding chores, the riders on the periphery started round again, and this time a horseshoe was hurled over a neighbouring building. It sailed through the air unobserved by the rather tense smokers and effectively knocked a corner out of the window glass behind them.

Annie heaved up the window and held it while she shook with angry passion. The swarthy man beside Mike sought to ingratiate himself with Annie, offering to go see who had done it. Mike, for his part, thought the chap might be taking on a whole lot of trouble, if Annie took him up on his offer.

Shrugging mightily, Annie shook her head. 'Don't tangle with them, Tony. They're scum.' Her angry eyes eventually turned dreamy. 'But if you ever see one of 'em in the saloon, a galoot with a long droopin' black moustache an' an eye that don't always follow the other, slip away an' tell me. I might be more than passin' grateful.'

Mike moved away far enough to watch one spirited ride through by the off duty labourers, but none of them looked particularly like his notion of a McArthur or a McAllen, and he retired to his rather high (and tightly tucked-in) single bed at an early hour, his mind brooding over the apparent fear which had shown in the eyes of Molly O'Callan at the mention of a man who might be her kin.

4

Punctually at noon the following day, Prusse's sweating labourers threw down their mallets, pegged out the mules and discarded their coils of telegraph wire. There was a throaty roar as they assembled at the mess hut with their battered plates and eating utensils for a meal built around beef stew.

From the food line they hurried to the long tables and hastily seated themselves to devour the food. Few men wore shirts, but all of them wore head coverings as protection against the all-powerful sun.

Wally's Wagon had been on the work site for almost an hour, but such was the uncertainty of Prusse's temper that Simmons had not ventured to suggest a time for selling their gear. Somehow, Kauffman managed to get his food early, and that meant he was a few minutes ahead of the hoggish eaters who formed his work crew.

Any sort of a shop wagon had its attraction, so Kauffman sidled along there while the men were still busy in the dining tent, and came to a tacit agreement with Simmons and Higgs for the half hour after food was consumed.

'You have to give them a half hour off after the meal, otherwise the poor jaspers would go loco, an' that would be the end of this venture for the Boss an' myself. So, I say, any who want to buy ordinary things like toilet requisites should be allowed to do so. Mostly they play cards after the food, or lie down an' sleep.'

Simmons thanked him kindly for his co-operation and Higgs slipped him a couple of good cigars. On the way back to the big tents, Kauffman perceived the arrival of yet another stranger: moreover, one who was definitely not expected. It was, in fact, the elderly constable from Pecos Town, who had conversed with Mike Liddell the previous evening. Constable Theo Savage came right on as if he had been sent along specifically to clear out the whole outfit single-handed.

Kauffman stood his ground. 'Shucks, Theo, you don't look like yourself no more. Me, I ain't ever seen you afore today without a grin on your face. Right now, you got an expression like you was seekin' your Pa's murderer.'

Savage checked his dun horse. 'There's been a stir up, Heinz. County sheriff has had a go at the marshal, told him this neck of the woods is Pecos Town property as far as peace-keepin' is concerned, an' someone in town with a lot of influence says there ought to be more arrests, more fines paid, if the marshal, the deputy an' me want to stay in a job. So I'm takin' the blame this far, bein' the lowly constable. Right?'

Kauffman took the constable off to the mess tent and insisted on him eating a meal. Meanwhile, the fastest eaters came out and inspected a few lines which the salesmen had to offer. Food tins did not go well, on account of the recent meal, and strong drink was a thing the manager disapproved of. Nevertheless, Higgs and Simmons turned over a few dollars, and Higgs seemed surprised when his older partner appeared to be discouraging custom.

'What you tryin' to do, Rufe? Get us a bad name?'

Simmons shushed him. 'No, I want to get close to this McArthur fellow, if I can. Thought I'd offer him a bottle of hair tonic. What do you think? I 'eard 'is hair was gettin' sort of thin!'

Higgs came near to throwing a fit, until Simmons allowed him to sniff the hair tonic and he found out that it was whisky.

For the gift of a comb, a hairy Scandinavian worker went into the recreation marquee and roused out Quentin McArthur. Troubled by the heat, McArthur was in a doubtful temper. He came straight up to the wagon with his thinning red hair hidden under his broad Tam-o'-shanter bonnet and a big belt and sporran across the front of his soiled bibbed overalls. Inserting his head through the opening in the side of the wagon, he glared at first one and then the other.

'Which of you two ornery north American hombres is makin' rude remarks about my hair? Or the lack of it?'

He was a formidable man, his forearms showing clearly his muscular strength. Wally Higgs flinched away from him, but Simmons slowly uncorked the hair tonic and held it under the Scot's whiskery nostrils. The two pseudo salesmen witnessed a most unusual change in McArthur's vindictive expression. From exuding menace it slowly changed to one of beaming pleasure.

'I see what you mean, gents! But why the hell didn't you come out into the open an' say what it was you had to sell? After all, no self-respectin' Scot would turn down an offer such as you're makin' to me.'

Simmons' countenance, so often exuding malevolence, matched the Scot's outgoing warmth. 'In the first place, Mr McArthur, the manager ain't all that keen on us sellin' strong liquor, an' in the second place we don't have much hair tonic left. So, you'll stick around an' drink it slowly, won't you?'

McArthur withdrew his head, and nodded without enthusiasm: as if drinking it slowly might be something of a task.

'How much 'll it be?'

Simmons hesitated. 'Well, to a McArthur, that little dose of medicine will be free. You'll owe me a favour sometime.'

The Scot thanked him, went round the back of the wagon and gave himself a preliminary snort from the bottle neck. As it burned its way down his throat, he shuddered a little and then straightened up again. Clearly, this was too good for him to drink all by himself. Dodging the salesmen's heads as they appeared at the counter, he hurried back to the recreation tent, and called to his partner from the flap.

'Hey, McAllen, will you come out here a minute? It . . . it's important!'

The Irishman was deeply involved in a game of cards with three glowering Germans he dearly wanted to beat. He looked up with his jaw muscles clenched and his close-set brown eyes showed intense displeasure.

'It had better be important, Jock, my lad, 'cause I've got a winnin' hand here.'

McAllen rose to his feet, having put down his cards, face downwards. He excused himself and hurried to the tent flap. 'What in tarnation are you tryin' to do, Jock? I — '

He paused as he smelled a whiff of his friend's breath. Quentin looked him straight in the eye, and showed the bottle he was holding.

'I've been offered a first class remedy for fallin' hair. There isn't a lot of it about, so I couldn't see me leavin' you out of it. You want to step out of the tent for a minute or two, or is your game of cards more important?'

McAllen grinned. His expression showed that his thoughts were racing. He was a greedy man at heart. He would dearly have liked to swig most of what was left in the bottle, and also win from the German card players all they had in the way of ready cash.

He winked at McArthur. 'Wait for me.' Stepping back inside, he drew himself up, formally, and addressed his fellow players. 'Gents, I'll be absent myself for two, or possibly three minutes. No more. Kindly roll yourselves a cigarette from the tobacco in my sack. And, be patient.'

He hoped he sounded firm enough to keep them from switching around the cards in his absence. On the other side of the big tent, the Irishman gurgled two or three fingers down his throat. Passing the bottle back to Jock, he murmured: 'It was good of you to think of your old buddy, Quent. Real good!'

McArthur nodded with his eyelids, being otherwise engaged. Slowly but surely, turn for turn, they emptied the bottle and together witnessed a development in the heat haze above the ground caused by their intake of neat spirit.

McAllen drank the last drops, held up the empty bottle and solemnly burped.

'All good things come to an end, old Irish buddy,' McArthur remarked with a yawn. The blazing sun was striking the back of his neck. McAllen drew him inside. 'When I've finished fleecin' these European card playin' gents, I'll have nice things to say to you. Now, why don't you go over there an' talk to the gent whose ridden all the way from town to talk to us. I — I won't be long!'

The friends parted. McArthur went a little way to where Constable Savage was eating the last of his lunch. On the way there, his legs felt heavy. Before he arrived, he found himself taking a dislike to the way in which the food disappeared under the sprouting moustache. He said as much, in a garbled fashion, and gracefully folded up at the foot of a stout supporting pole.

Meanwhile, McAllen had returned to the card players with a supercilious smile on his face. Privately, he thought they had taken far too much of his tobacco, but he kept it to himself. On three sides, he was aware of their bovine grins and mouths leaking acrid smoke.

Something went wrong with his winning hand. He remonstrated with his fellow players. At first he hinted that someone might have altered the cards around while he was away from the table. One player stood up, accepting the insult on behalf of all three. McAllen swung a punch at him, missed, and struck another player.

After that, he called out his accusations and threatened to take on the whole room, the telegraph company and all, if he didn't get satisfaction. Inevitably, men not in the game and the original fight joined in. Hard deal furniture was smashed. One pole was split, and the management in the shape of Kauffman and Prusse came in with a long club and two hand guns to back up their authority.

By the time Kauffman had cracked McAllen behind the ear, and sufficient witnesses had pointed out who started the trouble, the so-called tonic bottle had been smashed, and Constable Theo Savage hadn't got the right sort of patience to make an investigation at the end of the work line.

Higgs, who went to collect the mules, brought them back with his head discreetly out of sight between them, because a heated discussion between Prusse and his foreman as to whether the disgraceful McAllen would ever be allowed back on the site to work, almost ended in the two top men parting company for good.

Having put the animals in the shafts, Higgs scrambled back into the wagon where Simmons had been hiding since the riot began. He found his sidekick watching the tail end of the proceedings through a glass panel on the rear door, and chuckling to himself.

'I don't think what you've done was at all clever, Rufe!' the youthful gunman protested. 'McAllen is bein' taken off to jail, an' probably won't return, an' McArthur's sleepin' off the effects of the booze you gave 'im. 'Ow all this is goin' to 'elp Miss Melindy-Lou with 'er problems, I don't rightly know. Do you?'

Simmons chuckled some more, and jabbed Higgs in the ribs. 'You're takin' life too seriously, again, my son. As like as not, Melindy-Lou won't be interested in these jaspers. 'Er main interest is keepin' Charles Guerin from bein' the principal actor in a necktie party.

'Now, ain't that true? As for us, well, we won't want to be salesmen much longer, eh? We may get a call to do a bit of shootin' in some spot further east. Besides, if McAllen is in jail, we'll know where 'e is, won't we? That means we won't have to keep one eye open all the time to follow 'is movements.'

While they were talking, the hunched riding figure of Constable Theo Savage started on the return journey back to Pecos Town. He was pouting his lips to make his moustache stand out further, and his wide-brimmed hat was pulled down as far as possible to shield his ears from the foul, blasphemous and derogatory utterances of the man on the horse behind him.

McAllen had been permitted the freedom to use his hands and control his mount, but a tethering rope had been passed under the horse's belly from one of his boots to the other. He was in a more vicious mood than his language and his expression communicated.

'There he goes,' Higgs commented, unnecessarily.

'An' here comes the manager. Now, I want you to make a great effort to keep your face straight when I explain about that fool of a Scotsman drinkin' a bottle of liquid expressly made for scalp tonic. If you spoil my recital, I'll brand you, after the event!'

Higgs noted his partner's expression and the way in which he fiddled with his hidden knife. Clearly, Simmons meant it.

★   ★   ★

Meanwhile, in Pecos Town, Mike Liddell had been treating his self-imposed duties without undue exertion. After breakfast at Big Annie's he had wandered around the new developing settlement studying the new businesses, having a look at the people who were investing in the place and generally keeping a lookout for Scots and Irishmen.

On account of his vigilance, he had been about when a rider from the sheriff's office in that other developing part of the county, the county seat, arrived in town on the back of a pinto pony which had been ridden hard. The newcomer was merely a constable on the county sheriff's staff, but the paper which he brought with him expressly for the town marshal certainly caused a stir.

Mike was across the street when the marshal lost his temper and his raucous voice began to boom into the thoroughfare through the open window, and the door which had remained ajar.

The travelling constable took the full force of the marshal's displeasure after the full contents of the message had been digested by the veteran marshal, who only read letters when he was forced to and with the aid of spectacles. The messenger came out red-faced, having been told to go and take nourishment until the reply was ready.

Curious sidewalk loafers grinned at his dusty highly-coloured complexion, and yet he did not look at all cowed. In fact, from time to time he flashed looks of real venom in the direction of those who appeared to derive pleasure at his discomfiture.

Keeping in the shadow, Mike stuck his foot on the rail, and wondered if there was more trouble to come. As he had been intending to pass the time of day with the marshal, he felt that now the time would not be appropriate. His first stogie of the day was half way smoked when the town's deputy marshal started to approach from the east end of town, stepping jauntily and whistling as he came.

Rory Nevins was a thin-featured thirty year old, back as a civilian after five years as a corporal in the U.S. cavalry. He was a little above average height, tidily built, and light on his feet. The freshness of his complexion showed through his sunburn. His narrow moustache and short sideburns were a rich black colour. He had on a blue shirt, black trousers and a red bandanna. A further touch of colour showed in his cream stetson, which was pointed in the brim over his nose.

The whistling stopped as the deputy entered the office. There was a marked silence for five seconds or more, and then the marshal started to sound off about the sheriff's letter and the underhanded jasper who had been carrying messages to the county seat, saying that the standard of peace-keeping was low in Pecos Town.

Nevins protested lightly at first, then his voice took on an ominous boom. 'Now, see you here, marshal! I don't need this job if I don't like it, an' I don't like the way you're talkin' to me right now! So help me, I can rejoin the army any time I like, an' I don't have to take this from you!'

The marshal's answer had the volume, but not the resonant clarity.

Nevins resumed: 'Why would I be wantin' your job, for goodness' sake? I don't even know if I like my own yet!'

The slanging match went on for perhaps three more minutes. At the end of that time, the door opened and the deputy came out and paused, removing his hat and mopping his brow with the colourful bandanna.

'Where am I goin'? I'm makin' a patrol, if anybody asks! I'll be about the town!'

Nevins strode purposefully towards the west. On his travels, he met Theo Savage, who did not like to start work too early, and poor Savage took a worse verbal broadside from the marshal than the deputy had done. Unfortunately, he had not got the wit to withstand the torrent of words, and by that time Marshal Van Walters had thought of a few specific things for him to do. Consequently, Savage made his noteworthy visit to the end of telegraph, starting out less than fifteen minutes after the first intimation.

In his absence, the marshal and the deputy did more leg work than they had done ever since they were appointed, and all the time they steered clear of one another. Late in the afternoon, Nevins ran out his buckskin horse to save his legs.

Shortly afterwards, Mike Liddell

collected his chestnut and arranged to make contact with the deputy as the latter slowly rode the buckskin around the widening properties.

The Beauclerc man found that Deputy Nevins had long since stopped feeling a grievance. Moreover, he was glad of someone new with a different viewpoint with whom to pass the time of day.

Consequently, Mike mentioned that he had a sort of security job in Sundown, and that the folks he was in contact with were on the lookout for two men, one from Ireland and the other from Scotland.

A string of Irish oaths carried to them as they rode their mounts side by side, and wondered where to go for a convivial drink. Almost at once, Constable Savage and his prisoner, Paddy McAllen, came into view on two plodding horses.

Nevins was so surprised to see Savage with a prisoner that for a moment he was silenced. Mike leaned across and touched his reins.

'About that Irishman, Rory,' he began.

Nevins groaned. 'Yer, I know. While he's in jail, I'll try to find out what his future movements are, if he's likely to get out again in the near future.'

The drinking was postponed.

5

For an hour after the untimely departure of Constable Savage and his
unruly prisoner, Paddy McAllen, the
immediate fate of Wally's Stores, in
relation to the telegraph working gang,
hung in the balance.

Rufe Simmons did not give a hang
whether Gunther Prusse ordered them
away for good, and Wally Higgs merely
felt unsettled.

Prusse had said his piece, as soon as
the riding pair went off the premises.
He had said rude things in his
stilted north American English and
then relapsed into his native tongue,
German. This had given Simmons, who
was on the receiving end of the vicious
tirade, a chance to look vacant and put
on an innocent act.

Eventually, Simmons excused himself, stepped out of the rear door of the

wagon and went through a brief dumb show, as if the manager did not understand the native tongue. He took off his flat, rounded hat, indicated his hair which was thinning at the crown, and mimed the rubbing on of liquid from a bottle similar to that one from which McArthur and McAllen had drunk.

Just at the point when Prusse looked as if he might get the bottle from the miming salesman and hit him with it, the noisy pestilential signal to resume blasted their ears and effectively blanked out two angry exchanges. The work force moaned.

Oddly enough, Prusse was the first to give up. The constable and his prisoner were already out of sight, and in the near distance the men — albeit reluctantly — were swarming back to work without having to be driven out of the recreation marquee. The heat was smiting the manager through the back of his coat and making him perspire, a thing which he tried really hard to postpone as long as possible in the day while operating at the end of wire. Holding the bottle firmly in his right hand, the irate manager turned away from the salesman and hurried back to his tent, where he flopped down heavily into his seat and once again went over the reasons which had driven him to take a remote job such as this, so far away from the rest of mankind.

He did some accounting, checked the weekly rate of progress against certain distances marked on a crude map, and fell to wondering about the bottle. He supposed that some forms of hair tonic had an alcoholic base. There had been occasions in his own career when unusual booze substitutes had been welcomed by thirsty soldiers.

He wondered for a while longer, blinked at the low level of liquid in his bottle and decided to try a sample of the stuff which had apparently knocked out the Scotsman and made a raving lunatic out of his Irish sidekick.

It smelled fine. A mere soupçon on the tongue confirmed that it was the best sort of whisky to be found in the U.S. of A. Either whisky was a first class remedy for falling hair, or the two salesmen were cunningly peddling it under a false name. A second drink assured him that his original findings were accurate, and he was about to help himself to a third measure when Heinz Kauffman whistled in a certain way, and approached the tent.

Prusse would have liked time in which to hide the excellent liquor, even if its distribution against rules had caused trouble, but Kauffman entered too quickly, saw the bottle and adopted his most quizzical expression.

Kauffman seated himself, slightly ahead of the invitation and, averting his eyes, spoke out. 'Mr Rufe Simmons, manager of Wally's Stores, announces his regrets about the recent disturbance, for which he might be inadvertently to blame. He says one of his mules picked up a stone on the way here, and that's weakened one of its legs. Could they stay somewhere close, possibly for the night, if they kept strictly within the rules an' didn't open up without you first askin' 'em to do so?'

Having delivered himself of the longest speech of the day, Kauffman sagged and groaned. He received his measure of hair tonic with a modest nod and tackled it with greater alacrity than his superior.

'Here's to the hair on your chest, Gunther!' he sang out boldly.

The reception was cooler than he had expected, and so he hastily reworded his toast to only include his own chest. As he drank he lowered his eyes and massaged his cauliflower ear, as though the motion would help his drinking arrangements.

No immediate attempt was made to remove Wally's wagon from the area.

★ ★ ★

Evenings in the telegraph camp tended to become boring to the rank and file workers. Some men could sing quite tunefully, others got by in a chorus, on campfire songs and traditional melodies from their native lands. Of instrumentalists, there were few. Perhaps two men could play the mouth-harp, or Jews' harp, as it is called in some countries, and one other performed on the harmonica. There were three stringed instruments, of which the rather battered banjo was the most popular. The banjo kept tired singers singing longer than any other instrument.

Those who were short on stamina, or who had the habit of retiring early, sometimes fell asleep in the recreation marquee. Consequently, the protracted sleep of Quentin McArthur, which had caused him to miss the afternoon shift of work did not merit much conjecture during the evening hours of free time. Someone covered him with a canvas sheet before retiring to the sleeping quarters, and nothing of any description disturbed the wrong-doer until the early hours.

★　★　★

About a furlong away from the main tented settlement, Simmons and Higgs were in a far from restful mood. They had partaken of liquor from their dwindling stock, played several hands at cards, until the dwindling light took some of the fun out of the proceedings, and then grudgingly erected their lean-to tent, which hooked onto the side of the vehicle.

Higgs was slow to turn in, on the ground. 'I don't know why we're 'angin' about here, Rufe. After all, this business of McArthur an' McAllen, it ain't all that important compared with Melindy-Lou an' the Frenchman who don't want to swing. Is it, now? Why are we wastin' our lives out 'ere in the wilderness, 'cause that's what it is, neither more nor less.'

Simmons, who had found a rather

more suitable piece of ground for his sleeping arrangements, and also had won at cards, saw the situation in a different light. 'Boy, if you want to be an outlaw for a long period an' if your ambition is to stay out of trouble, you got to 'ave patience. Out this way, no snoopin' lawman is goin' to take a close look at us, an' that's a good thing, 'cause if we're ever goin' to stay useful to Melindy-Lou we 'ave to stay away from trouble.

'Any persistent peace officer comes hot on our trail, she won't want to know us, 'cause we'd only lead trouble to 'er an' she wouldn't want that!'

Higgs rolled himself again in his blanket, groaning a little to himself and knowing he had not the words with which to refute Simmons' argument.

'Hey, hello there!'

The croaking voice from beyond the small area illuminated by a turned-down lamp at once alerted the two desperadoes. With an unusual scissor-like action, Higgs grabbed for his twin guns, which nestled under his flattened black hat that doubled as a pillow. Simmons' knife slid down his forearm into his hand almost like a reflex action, while his questing free hand located a gun. He rolled onto his chest, frowned at his partner, and cleared his throat.

'Who is it?'

'It's me, Quentin. The Scotsman. Seems I've been asleep for quite a number of hours. I can't seem to get any sense or sympathy out of the workin' team. So I took a walk, an' I saw your lamp. Is it too late to talk?'

Simmons groaned audibly. Privately, he thought that perhaps Higgs was right about their wasting time out there, in the open, but he did not say as much. 'Come on in, Quentin. You'll want to know about your buddy, McAllen.'

In spite of his feeling out of sorts with himself, McArthur mustered a show of interest when McAllen's name was mentioned. While he tentatively picked over some cold, unappetising food, they told him of Paddy's demise and the way in which the disgruntled constable had taken him off to town.

'I'll no stay here without him, not even to collect my wages, an' that's a fact,' the Scot remarked, his fingers busy with his thinning hair. 'He's helped me on occasion, an' I'll be after doin' the same for him. When will you be headed back for town?'

There was a lot of yawning. The partners avoided making a careful statement, but somehow or another, while the coffee pot was simmering, they got around to the idea of actually moving off without waiting for daylight. Quentin's hangover did not deprive him of energy, and when he elected to collect and harness the mules, the energies of the other two were fully restored.

No one from the main camp appeared to question their night departure and the journey back to town did not appear to be a long one because McArthur made up for his many somnolent hours by talking a great length about Scotland, Scottish high-land games, and the engaging prospects at the Chateau Beauclerc for a man from overseas whose relation knew *la Baronne* well.

More whisky accounted for the Scot's loquacity, but not for the increasing restlessness which possessed him as the weighty wagon rolled back into town under a greying sky. He became impatient as the partners slowed down at the west end of Main Street between the first of the series of false fronts, and when they showed no signs of speeding up to take him to the peace office, he rather hurriedly dropped out of the tail door, curtly thanked them and parted company.

Within three minutes, the Scot was knocking on the door of the peace office. The wagon was stationary. Simmons, chewing on a small wad of tobacco, awaited the return of Higgs from an errand the latter thought superfluous at that time of the morning. The young gunman had been sent to the recently opened telegraph office to see if there was any message for them.

McArthur's anger soon boiled up in the peace office. He was confronted by a sleepy Theo Savage, who informed him that the Irishman was in a cell at the rear, cooling off against a possible charge for being drunk and disorderly.

Savage had his stockinged feet resting on the top of the marshal's desk, along with his hat and shotgun. The rest of his body was draped over the spacious swivel chair. McArthur, having had his begrudged explanation, loomed up in front of the desk and waved a broad index finger in the constable's face.

'You can't hold him for bein' drunk an' disorderly where there is no proper community, so you're curtailin' his liberty unfairly!'

Savage shrugged and massaged his moustache which felt like an unwatered plant. 'So come back in office hours an' explain your legal reasonin' to the head man!'

'You canna give back a man's time!

Nobody can put the clock back, constable!' Changing the tone of his voice, and shouting, Jock turned in the direction of the cell block door. 'Are you in there, Paddy? This is Jock callin' you!'

'Yer, I'm here, Jock! The bed's hard, my stomach's empty an' I figure the breakfast will be late an' scarcely eatable!'

The two men eyed one another from a yard or so apart. Quentin grinned unexpectedly. 'Release him into my custody, constable! I'll bring him back after breakfast.'

The suggestion had the opposite of the desired effect. 'If you don't clear out, Scotsman, I'll take you into custody, as well. For disturbin' the peace in this town's quiet hours! Do you understand me?'

Savage eased the butt of the shotgun nearer to him, and lowered his feet to the floor, knocking over his boots. He had turned mean again. McArthur backed off. He would not take on an angry man with a shotgun, but he had not given up. He left the office, and moved resolutely to another location.

Meanwhile, Higgs had found several messages which had not been claimed fixed to the inside of the telegraph office window, so that their purport could be read from the street. He had burned his hand when his first match stick burned low without his noticing it.

He struck another, coaxed it at the spluttering birth, and applied himself to the message for a second time. It read:

To Rufus Higgs, Pecos Town.
Goods may arrive Sunrise ahead of schedule. Keen traders expected county seat quite soon.
M. L. Enterprises.

Higgs ran all the way back to the wagon, mouthing over the gist of the message continuously. When he arrived he needed a drink before he could repeat it sensibly, and his memory took a knock for a minute or more.

'So we ought to be movin' for Sunrise real soon,' Simmons opined.

He found the message stimulating and full of interest, but his lack of sound sleep made him irritable. Meanwhile, the resolute Scot — having made his way to the rear of the peace office by a roundabout route — contemplated with interest some stout posts left by builders in a tidy heap. His mind at once flashed to his favourite sport: that of caber-tossing. The fence at the rear of the peace office was not complete. An outrageous, hairbrained plan made him grin, chuckle and think that his frustrations could shortly be brought to an end.

The constable was alone in the office still. McArthur studied the wooden door facing him on the end of the cell block. He thought a well-tossed caber would knock it in quite effectively. And so it was that the fanatical Scot began his assault upon the rear of the cells.

McAllen was wide awake enough to

cheer as the first pole hit the centre of the rear door with an ominous blow strong enough to shake the hinges. The Scot backed away from the first one, muttering to himself and altogether ignoring the constable who was shouting angrily through the window in the rear of the office.

Other shouts came from the area beyond the fence, in what would one day, no doubt, be called Second Street. McAllen was slow to make any remark, but the sounds through his cell grille suggested he was moving about.

'Do it fast, or else give up, Jock! They're liable to put you away forever!'

McArthur carried on his routine as though his actions were quite unnoticed. He was oblivious to the shouts and protests that grew around him. Men peered carefully from all the vantage points round about, and nearly a score were close enough to see the end of the second caber clout the door in the weakened spot. The door in question shuddered, looked as if it might withstand the second assault then abruptly caved inwards, leaving the hinges and collapsing like a drawbridge.

The Scot filled his chest, gave out with an unearthly highland cry of triumph and collapsed on his chest in his death throes.

Those who had witnessed the incredible sight to date, peered around at one another and then further afield. All had heard the crack of the bullet, but no one seemed to be sure from which direction it had come.

The crowd trebled itself. Several women and a young boy had joined it. Van Walters came through from the office, walking gingerly over the fallen timber with Savage at his heels. Rory Nevins, the deputy, ran in from the other direction, panting a little and holding a Colt revolver across his chest.

Mike Liddell, who had slept reasonably well at Big Annie's, arrived breathlessly about a minute later. By that time, a patch of blood had seeped through the work overall, under the victim's left arm.

Deputy Nevins confirmed to Mike that the victim was the Scot, known as Quentin McArthur, and that none of the peace officers had anything to do with the fatal bullet.

6

The news that the population had gone down by one soon spread around Pecos Town, and fed the imagination of the earliest town settlers. Uppermost in the minds of those who liked sensation was the unheard of method used by the Scotsman to effect an entry to the jail.

No one had ever heard of a single man using a light tree bole as a battering ram to knock in a door. Such things had been used in the west to assault the stout wooden doors which gave entrance to remote army forts, and others had been used to breech the entrance to a prison, on occasion; but to break into an ordinary town peace office in order to spirit away a single inmate, a man only in there for the mild crime of disturbing the peace and maybe using threatening language. Never . . .

Quentin McArthur had been hit and killed by a rifle bullet fired from an unknown distance away. His apparent murder at once prompted a search of the area. No one, so it seemed, had attempted to assist the appointed peace officers by shooting the man breaking into the cell block.

The marshal, the deputy and the constable all went in different directions. Mike Liddell, with a harsh scowl on his otherwise scarcely-lined face, prowled about on his own.

McArthur was foolish, nay reckless in his actions but not many people who witnessed what he was up to would want to blast him just for being a nuisance to the law enforcement officers. Mike found himself wondering if anyone knew where he was headed for. If McArthur was in the habit of taking scotch whisky, he would probably be a talkative fellow. Probably several of his workmates knew he was going to Sundown City, and that his kinsman had connections with the family at the chateau. *But why should he be killed?*

Mike stayed away from his breakfast at Big Annie's and spent upwards of two hours moving around the town, looking in some buildings, observing others from the outside. He stood about, listening to groups and weighing up their conversation, but his private investigations took him no nearer a solution of the problem shooting.

Gradually, the sun mounted the sky and the heat took its toll of the searchers. Eventually, normal working was more or less resumed. Two things had surprised Mike. The first was that only two men from the telegraph gang appeared to be in town. They were, of course, the constable's Irish prisoner and the Scotsman who had been shot.

The only other item of special interest was the telegraph message pinned to the window of the new telegraph office, and addressed to someone named Rufus Higgs, in Pecos

Town. Goods arriving ahead of schedule in the new county seat could mean anything. It was the tailpiece that interested him. 'M. L. Enterprises.' Some sort of business house with the same initials as his own. Unless it was in a code of some sort.

He brooded over the message through his late breakfast in a cafe. Not even an extra cup of excellent coffee stirred his imagination to a worthwhile solution of the puzzle. A call on the telegraph clerk failed to clear it up, as well.

After a time, Mike grew tired of speculating about others. He began to see the McArthur business through the eyes of his friend, old Jock McArthur, the veteran blacksmith of Sundown. How on earth would he — the accredited troubleshooter from the big house — be able to look his old friend in the face and admit that he had been murdered almost under his very nose, a mere few days' ride from his destination?

While he pondered, others did the same, unknown to him.

★   ★   ★

Simmons and Higgs came up from the creek when the early searching was over. It was easy for them to acquire a few facts about the demise of Paddy McAllen. In fact, they were as surprised as anyone else at the unexpected outcome deriving from their having brought McArthur back into town.

Their eyes took in the thoughtful figure of Mike Liddell after the latter had tired somewhat in his abortive search and gone in upon himself.

Simmons' first reaction was to smile so widely that his broad features appeared to be in two halves. He crooked up his forearm and felt the tip of the throwing knife tickling his skin. Higgs did not have his twin holsters with him, and all he wanted to do was to backtrack to the wagon and tool up.

The rotund Simmons agreed with

him at first. Liddell could be eliminated, by them. A nice bit of justice for the way in which he had eluded them in a clash on a train. Revenge would be sweet . . .

But on the way back to the wagon, which they had hidden in sparse trees beside the diminutive creek, the older man began to have second thoughts.

'I'm not so sure, Wally,' he confided, as they reached the shelter of the trees.

Higgs, perspiring in a black gunman's outfit, pulled up short and mopped his brow on a soiled grey handkerchief. Simmons likewise dabbed the red mark across his brow, left by the pressure of his stiff-brimmed hat.

'You ain't talkin' of backin' out on a bit of revenge play, are you, Rufe?'

Simmons chewed on tobacco. He was slow to answer. 'You make it sound like I'm a coward, Wally, an' that ain't nice. Especially when I've taught you all you know about livin' on the wrong side of the law. It may be better if we stay away from Liddell on this one occasion. I'll spell it out for you.

'We've just had an urgent coded message warnin' us to get to Sunrise without delay. Now, so far we haven't complied with that request. Another thing. If Liddell is tryin' to drum up trouble in Pecos Town, he ain't in a place where he can do Melindy-Lou any harm. See what I mean?'

Higgs emerged from the wagon fingering his heavy gun belt and its appendages. He nodded, showing a lot of ill felling.

'I suppose it wouldn't do to draw attention to ourselves, in this two mule town, even accidentally. When we're supposed to be some place else. So what do we do? Hadn't we better clear out right away?'

'Yer. I don't feel all that energetic, an' it's been kind of homely, ridin' around on that wagon. Still, I figure the time has come when we ought to part company with it. In case, in case it leads anyone to us whose company we can do without.'

Keeping a sharp watch on the direction of town, they settled in the shade and began to make plans for leaving. At first, they quarrelled about details, but as they passed a small lighted cigar from one to the other they found a basis of agreement.

Their best plan seemed to be to clear town in a roundabout fashion, so as not to attract any sort of attention. After that, they would look for a suitable spot where an accident could happen to the wagon. The mules, of course, could still be of use until they saw an opportunity to acquire some decent horses. Perhaps they could hang on to one of the hybrid animals to carry some of the useful stock still in the wagon.

As they finalised their plans, Higgs became restless again. He wanted to send a simple coded message to Melindy-Lou in Sundown, to tell her that Mike Liddell was in Pecos Town. Against his better judgement, Simmons reluctantly agreed to such a scheme. It meant that the two of them

96

had to part for a while.

Higgs had a long face when he came back. He had sent the message they had spent time over, but there had been no reply. All they could conclude was that the lady in question had already left Sundown City, presumably on her way to Sunrise. After that, they dawdled no more.

★　★　★

About the time when Quentin McArthur was indulging in his second caber-tossing exhibition away from his native land, and at the same time achieving his last long sleep, Town Marshal Abel Smith of Sundown City, was awakened early and handed a message from the county seat.

It intimated that the building programme in the new county town was coming to an end ahead of schedule. As a result, the matter of justice pending for the French prisoner incarcerated in a special cell in Sundown could now be dealt with so much sooner. In fact, a team of guards — recruited for the express purpose of moving the prisoner — would be arriving that very morning to take him to more permanent quarters, prior to his trial.

Consequently, Abel had stalked off along the street, been there ahead of the newcomers and had done everything he could to expedite the long tedious ride to Sunrise.

The lady who turned up at the same time as the guards, well-spoken and apparently French, surprised him a little at first, but when she explained that she had been sent along by the county attorney, to be in attendance en route, Abel had merely thought that times were changing. There was no denying that the Guerin character's wound was still not completely healed.

When Jock McArthur had snatched a Colt revolver and shot the Frenchman in the shoulder from close range during that other debacle outside the chateau, he had done a good job. The bullet had gone through the flesh of the escaping prisoner's right shoulder and made sure that he did not elude capture.

Some five or six miles away from Sundown City, riding east by northeast, the special posse of eight riders, plus the prisoner and the female in the short riding skirt, had settled down to a slow economic speed.

All the guards wore a uniform of sorts, inasmuch as they had been issued with a dark jacket and a light-coloured tall stetson apiece.

Two men, in particular, seemed to have a closer interest in the prisoner and the female who was never far from beside him. They were both mounted up on big dun horses and they had the appearance of men who had for long periods worked together. In fact, Hal Crowder, a homely big-boned westerner with thick red hair, matched in his sideburns and brows, was the nephew of the older man, Silas Warden, who was nearly twice his age. Warden's skin was seamed and deeply tanned.

The richness of its colouring was in deep contrast to his grey hair, which stuck out from the sides of his stetson.

Crowder was the one who finally made special contact with the lady rider. From his position in the lead, along with Warden, he contrived to slightly impede the mounts of the prisoner and the woman, who was a well-made shapely brunette. The exchanges between the prisoner and nurse, in the French language, at first speeded up and then were cut out altogether.

The woman complained. 'Hell, deputy, you may be totin' a prisoner an' the day may be hot, but you could at least give us room to ride along behind you without bein' impeded.'

Crowder chuckled. He glanced back to see if any of the other six riders bringing up the rear were paying special attention to the exchanges up front. Apparently, none were.

'I was doin' it on purpose, ma'am, so as to attract your attention!'

The nurse was wearing a wide-brimmed straw hat with a light veil. She adjusted the veil slightly so as to get a better glimpse of the impertinent fellow with the reddish brows and sideburns.

'Now I wonder why a temporary guard should want to get the attention of a travellin' female nurse? You ain't expectin' the prisoner to make a break for it, are you, with his hands secured to the saddle horn?'

Crowder cleared his throat. He winked at his older riding partner.

'No, not exactly, ma'am. But all those exchanges in the French language don't have to add up to whether his bonds are botherin' him. I figure you know him a whole lot better than folks around here are supposed to know. As a matter of fact, Silas Warden an' me, we're buddies an' relations. If we've summed up this prisoner aright, he's been in conflict with the folks at the French chateau.

'In a manner of speakin' so have we. We were employed as deputy an' constable in the town of Little Springs when a certain Mike Liddell came along there. He was suspected of havin' murdered some Mexican horse minders an' stolen a few fine lookin' horses.'

Clearly, the nurse's interest had quickened. So had that of the swarthy prisoner, who blinked his bulbous eyes and adopted his favourite expression: one which accentuated his lantern jaw and tightened his thin mouth. His knowledge of American English was far from lacking.

The woman said: 'Come to the point, deputy. If not, those at the rear may get suspicious. In fact, I'm a suspicious person, myself. I don't know if you're tryin' to set me up for something.'

Crowder ignored her. He went on: 'Warden, an' me, we were thrown out under suspicion, an' since then we've been on the lookout for an opportunity to get even with Liddell an' his employer. I'll spell it out for you. My pardner an' me, we'd be interested in a worthwhile proposition to help a prisoner who might have suffered through clashes with the Beauclerc setup.'

The nurse appeared to be studying the two forward riders again in the light of what she had just learned. The former Capitaine Charles Guerin intimated by a brief nod of the head that he was interested in the revelations.

Eventually, the shapely brunette spoke out. 'Supposin' there was something in your conjecture, Crowder, about this business an' a link-up with the Beauclerc family. In that case, I might be able to use you an' your buddy at some future date. But you'd have to lie low an' wait for instructions from me. An' you could be called upon to shoot upon such men as you ride with now.'

Crowder, who thought she must have seen his name in a newspaper report, nodded in tacit agreement. He admired the way she forked the horse, handicapped by a short riding skirt. He took her to be a woman with plenty of nerve, and he was right.

7

A helpless sense of foreboding bugged Mike Liddell. A feeling that forces were working against him. After contacting an undertaker new to the town and making arrangements for poor Quentin McArthur to be measured for his final outfit, a wooden one, he took the opportunity to join forces with Deputy Nevins who had been assigned the task of informing the manager of the telegraph crew what had happened to his two workers from the British Isles.

It was a dusty, unpleasant ride. As they jogged along on their respective horses, side by side, the dark-haired deputy did his best to make agreeable conversation, although privately he thought that his companion, the Sundown troubleshooter, was grubbing around looking for trouble where another man would have sidestepped any involvement.

In answer to a question, Nevins said: 'I don't think you'll find either Prusse, the manager, or Kauffman, the foreman, will express any serious regrets. Shucks, McArthur and McAllen 're difficult characters, an' if they both drop out now, it won't matter, because there's a steady trickle of labour comin' in from Texas an' places further north.'

The peace officer looked as if he wanted to say more, but he held off. Prompted warmly by Mike, he added: 'I can't see why you didn't telegraph the bad news about McArthur's death before we left town, Mike. After all, they've got to know, sooner or later, an' it might be better, comin' from you, a friend.'

Mike groaned. 'You're right, Rory. Fact is, I'm very fond of old Jock, the blacksmith. That's why I put off tellin' them. I don't figure I'm very good at condolences. It's the sort of job for an older man. Besides, I'm completely baffled by the shootin' just the same as you are, an' the folks I work for an' live with, they'll expect me to offer a few explanations, even if I can't find the gunman.'

Nevins commiserated with his riding companion, and when they talked for a change about travel and riding horses the journey seemed shorter.

However, the interview in the manager's private tent was far from relaxed. The Boss heard of McArthur's demise without showing any particular interest. He displayed complete indifference as to whether McAllen should ever come back to work for him. He revealed not the slightest curiosity about the identity of the assassin and soon indicated by his attitude that his two visitors were wasting their own time, and his.

Mike flashed the irate manager an engaging smile of the type which had admitted him to some very select company on occasion. It was the sort of expression that wrinkled the corners of his blue eyes and made women glance at him a second time.

'Herr Prusse, Deputy Nevins an' I seem to have wasted your time. You have a time schedule to keep to, an' we ought to get out of your way. I'd like to ask one small favour before we leave. Would it be possible to send a telegraph message from here? Right from the end of the wire?'

Gunther Prusse slapped his riding breeches, frowning as he did so. He stood up, poker-faced and indifferent. His thirst was troubling him. He determined to be free of his visitors, regardless of how far they had ridden.

'Gentlemen, all that I can tell you that you don't seem to know already is that McArthur probably left here with the two travelling salesmen. The ones who came with the wagon, an' prolonged their stay because one of their mules was supposed to be incapacitated. I heard tell that they addressed one another as Rufe and Wally.

'They should be able to tell you a bit more about the Scotsman, although I can't think why you should be so interested in the fate of an ordinary immigrant workman from Europe. As to the other matter, my company are not keen for me to send messages in between towns. My next message will not be sent until we arrive at the river boundary. An' now, I must ask you to leave. I don't think McArthur had any personal possessions worth mentionin', or our business is concluded.'

All through this last speech, Mike Liddell had felt himself growing more and more annoyed. He had intended to ask if the Scotsman had any money to be collected, in unpaid wages, but something in the eyeglance of the deputy helped him to keep his protests in check, and the two of them left shortly afterwards, not even restored by a cup of coffee.

On the way back to town, Nevins tried his hand at a verbal description of the appearance of the man who called himself Wally, and his bulky, more mature travelling companion.

'That Wally is a tall thin young fellow.

Rather pale in the face. Tends to dress in black, like a certain type of gunman. His nostrils tend to twitch a lot, an' he has a hangdog look about him, as if he is always ready to drop into a certain type of crouch, if you know what I mean.'

Mike peered forward, watching the dust and stones on the trail beyond the twitching ears of the plodding chestnut horse. He knew what his companion meant, all right. Moreover, he had a sinking feeling in the pit of his stomach which seemed to suggest that he had clashed with this same young man before.

Rory went on. 'The other fellow Rufe, wasn't so tall. He would be about forty. Sort of rounded, an' muscular. Noisy breather as if 'e was over weight, but most of it was muscle, I'd say. Round-faced. Brown hair with a bald crown. Looked as if he ought to be a monk, only I wouldn't say he was an honest type at all. Or trustworthy. Used one of those hats with a very straight brim an' flat top. An' when he grinned — '

'His teeth were small, tobacco-stained an' widely spaced,' Mike put in, without waiting for the full description.

Rory rounded on him. 'You've met them before, Mike!'

'I believe I have. On a train, in the south of the county, it was, a few months back. Those boys are bad to tangle with, I can assure you. I'm really surprised to hear they went out to the camp with a wagon full of groceries. No one will convince me they've mended their ways. They could be the ones to eliminate a fellow like McArthur, although I still can't figure what their motive would be, in his case.'

Mike increased the pace for the rest of the ride back to Pecos. He had withdrawn into himself. He was blaming himself for having wasted quite a deal of time. The telegraph message ought to have been sent off to Sundown before he left town in the first place, and there was another item. Something connected with a piece of information he had seen. His memory refused to reveal what it was that he wanted to recall, and he found himself wondering if it had to do with bad tidings.

His inner thoughts made him less companionable on the last mile into town. So much so that he invited Nevins into the nearest saloon on arrival to quench his thirst.

A half hour later, he was visiting the telegraph office with a difficult message concocted in his mind. The clerk, a veteran of the type who kept moving west with the extension of wire, like a frontiersman, took his message, blinked at him from under his green eyeshade and nodded to show a modicum of sympathy.

He checked it, worked out its cost and went to work with his vital finger.

Molly O'Callan, c/o Beauclerc, Sundown City.
Please inform Jock McArthur of

*sad death of his kinsman in unfor-
tunate accident, Pecos Town. Am
working on it.*

Paddy McAllen in area.

Michael Liddell.

'You expectin' any sort of a reply, Mr
Liddell?'

'It's quite possible. I expect to be in
town all day. If you like I'll look in later,
this afternoon.'

After partaking of a modest meal,
Mike checked the town again for signs
of the pair described by Nevins. They
were nowhere to be found. No one
claimed to have seen them all day.
There was no sign of the travelling
wagon, either.

Feeling scarcely adequate for his
job, he retracted his steps to Big
Annie's establishment, made excuses
for being away without informing her
of his intentions, and retired to his
room where he threw himself on
the bed. There, minus his boots and
hat, he thought over his prospects

for the near future.

With the Rufe and Wally pair in the vicinity, and apparently staying out of sight, there was almost certain to be trouble. Mike had thwarted them in the last encounter. As they were obviously employed as killers, he had need to be very careful in the future.

Moreover, in the past they had been associated with a formidable woman who had two or three aliases. Those who had seen her talents as a dancer, singer and entertainer mostly knew her as Melindy-Lou. And that was where the M.L. coincidence occurred. He recollected then about having seen a telegraph message relating to M. L. Enterprises.

Could that mean anything other than *Melindy-Lou Enterprises*?

And the Rufus Higgs it was addressed to must have been one of the pair on the travelling wagon, who had worked for Melindy-Lou in the past!

Mike repeated the gist of the message attached to the telegraph office window.

He was so concerned about its apparent meaning that he sat up slowly and repeated it aloud.

He added: 'It's Melindy-Lou again, chancin' her arm to assist Charles Guerin! An' the keen traders in question will be on their way now.' He lowered his voice, although there was no one about to overhear. 'The goods in question could just possibly be Charles Guerin, himself.'

But if his conjecture so far was near the truth, then surely the authorities must have organised an earlier removal of the prisoner to the county seat. If that were so, did it mean the trial of Guerin had been brought forward?

After that, he was too disturbed to sleep. He walked up and down and finally had to leave the building around three o'clock. His toe which had been injured twitched in his new boot as he tramped back to the telegraph office on the offchance of a return message.

His knock aroused the clerk, who

pointed to the reply he was waiting for and indicated a seat.

Mike Liddell, Pecos Town.
Leave Quentin. Imperative you go direct to Sunrise pronto. Use McAllen. C.G. gone. Madame unwell.

McArthur.
Sundown City.

Mike rocked absently on the chair, tossing over a small cigar to the clerk, who did not intrude upon his private thinking.

Apparently Jock, himself, had sent the reply. The old Scot had made no mention at all about his feelings connected with the kinsman who had come so far and then lost his life when so near to his destination. Everything seemed to have gone out of focus.

Madeleine was unwell: probably suffering from a mild fever, which she seemed prone to since she settled in the territory. And Molly was worried about the character of Paddy McAllen, the fellow it was suggested he shoult take with him to Sunrise as an assistant, or back-up man of some sort.

He came to his feet slowly, fiddling with coins which he produced from his shirt pocket. As the clerk received them, Mike was thinking rather bitter thoughts. If only old Jock had shot Charles Guerin dead a few weeks back, instead of just wounding him. The county would have been saved a lot of time and trouble, and the Beauclerc people might have avoided a lot of worry and stress.

The heat hit him as he stepped out of the office. One thing was for sure. Pecos Town had just about seen the last of him for quite a time.

8

Standing in the shadow afforded by the side wall of the blacksmith's shop in the west end of Sundown City, Molly O'Callan looked calm and perhaps a trifle pale. She had on over her neat grey work dress a walking-out cloak with a becoming bottle-green cowl. Her auburn tresses appeared to sparkle in the bright light when she moved out of the shadow. She held an elegant basket in her two hands.

She pursed her full lips at times as she conversed with the bulky blacksmith who was on the point of leaving town.

'Jock, I can't tell you how distressed I am to learn of your cousin's death. Especially as he had arrived in the county. I don't believe Mike could have been in contact when it happened.'

'Don't distress yourself, Miss Molly.

The fellow who told me, ahead of the message, said a gunshot wound. But we'll see. Me, I hope you'll have more joy with your relation. Paddy McAllen, was it? I reckon he'll be along some time soon. Mike will see to that, even though they have to go to Sunrise first.'

Molly opened her mouth to speak, and then checked herself. Jock glanced at her curiously, adjusting his hat, as he did so. She contrived an uncertain smile, and he could see that she had other troubles on her mind.

'He's not a bad lot, is he?' Jock queried.

A nervous laugh from the Irish-woman. 'Well, he could be. How do people say? An eye to the main chance, is it? The sort of man who might — just might take up bounty huntin' or somethin' unsavoury to earn his daily bread. I'm not relishin' meetin' up with him, not at all, I'm not.'

There was a short silence before Jock replied. Molly looked shattered when he suddenly rumbled with laughter.

'Well, then, if he's *that* sort of a fellow, he'll no doubt be good with a gun! An' that will please Mike, who has to do most of the dirty work strictly on his own!'

Molly coaxed a suitable reply out of herself, but she soon relapsed into the grip of her inner worries when the old man had mounted up and started on the punishing horseback journey with only misery at the end.

The young woman went into a cafe and took coffee. All she could think of at the time was the safety of Mike Liddell. He had taken so many risks on behalf of them all, and sometimes only survived by a minor miracle. And now he had been advised to take along her kin, Paddy McAllen. The same Paddy that she and her cousin, Sheilagh, had given the slip shortly after arriving in the U.S.A.

Surely, Paddy couldn't have changed all that much in sixteen years. Wasn't she right to expect that he would take advantage of Michael, and of the

Beauclerc household, if he was given the chance? The prospect frightened her. More so than the early moving of that villain, Guerin, to the county seat.

She stopped licking her dry lips a minute or more after her cup was empty, recollected that Madeleine, *la Baronne*, was running a temperature and probably depressed by being on her own.

Once again, it seemed, the fortunes of those connected with the Beauclerc set-up hung in the balance.

★　★　★

The make-do settlement where the prisoner, Charles Guerin, was housed in transit, had formally been the offices and warehouse of an exploratory mining company, founded when the population of the territory was a whole lot thinner. Being situated scarcely more than three miles west of the new county seat, the cluster of wooden shacks had been deemed to be a useful and safe stopping place for a prisoner and escort far on in an important journey.

The biggest of the shacks was the one actually used to house Guerin while the men and the horses rested.

One of the guards had ridden on to the county seat to inform the sheriff and the officer of the court how the prisoner's journey was progressing, and when the outfit could be expected to arrive for the judge's hearing.

During the hottest part of the afternoon, all the remaining guards, with the exception of Hal Crowder and his elderly sidekick, Silas Warden, were glad to get their heads down in a siesta. The two who had privately contacted the travelling nurse were patrolling outside the key building, one on the gallery in front, and the other close along the wall in the rear.

Inside, Guerin was massaging his wrists and alternately complaining about his lot and threatening what was going to happen to his enemies in the event that he managed to get clear of the authorities on the following day.

Sitting in a corner between two windows, with her legs crossed and one airborn foot swinging rhythmically, Melindy-Lou, alias Marie-Louise, christened Manuella Sanchez, revealed her impatience by taking frequent drags at a small cigar and waving her arm in between times.

Guerin could not help but admire her shapely legs and the hour glass figure and imposing bosom which had started her into show business at an early age.

'With a little more culture, finish, shall we say, you could fit in with the best of company. High society, even.'

She knew that when he started to talk of her and her appearance that his confidence in this hastily assembled plan to free him must have grown. She chuckled to herself.

'For now, *mon brave*, you should stick to admiring the plan, not me. A great deal will depend upon our visitor.

If he fails to turn up there could be gun play, an' the outcome of that is always in doubt, as you know.'

Guerin, who had thought they might become very much better acquainted before concluding their enforced journey, grimaced.

'What, who is this visitor who is so . . . important to your plan, *mademoiselle*?'

'He is a man who used to work for a practising attorney in Sundown City. A man with experience of detective work, even if he was fired by the Pinkerton agency for some misdemeanour or another. A man who can be manipulated. Used for a day or so. One who will do as he is told, for cash reward, backed up possibly by fear.'

A sharp chuckle transformed the keen, sensuous expression on the Frenchman's face.

'You certainly have a way with men, Melindy. I hope he comes, but not straight away, eh?'

Before he had the time to explain

himself, or she had the time to protest, Hal Crowder had crossed the gallery and kicked the front door with his boot heel.

'A visitor on the way in, miss. A tall thin hombre on a grey bronc. Looks like an undertaker's man to me. Or an out-of-work drifter.' Crowder cleared his throat, dropped his voice, and went on in a more conciliatory tone. 'Of course, if he's a friend of yours, I'm sure Silas an' me will be quite civil to 'im.'

Melindy stepped briskly to the door in her stockinged feet.

'Anyone else around?' she whispered, having opened the door.

'No one *I* know about,' the over-confident redhead retorted.

Side by side, they watched the arrival of the shifty-looking newcomer. His long frame was hunched in the saddle. The thin black moustache drooped on either side his narrow mouth, partially shielding his hollow, pale cheeks. He wore a tall undented hat and a suit which had also been black before he put the shine on it.

The rider frowned, his eyes slitted, at his reception committee, before crossing over and dismounting by the gallery. He appeared to wheeze slightly due to the exertion of lowering himself to the ground. Crowder was impressed by the pair of Colt revolvers in worn holsters. He thought that it was possible to underestimate their latest acquaintance.

'Good day, I'm Clint Brant, although the name is not generally known in these parts.'

He reached up and touched his hat, at the same time giving off a slight odour of perspiration. Crowder and Melindy-Lou exchanged glances before the woman smuggled the newcomer indoors. The guard looked as if he would have liked to be a witness to the interview, but Melindy easily convinced him that he ought to stay out of doors and in sight of anyone on the prowl.

Brant acted as though he was at ease

until he saw the Frenchman indoors with the lethal expression. He nevertheless removed his hat and squatted on the edge of the chair, which Melindy pushed forward for him.

'Now, Brant, apart from me, no other person involved in this little matter knows how capable you are. Make your report.'

Having reseated herself, the dominating young woman contemplated him through a fine plume of smoke. Guerin, who was too restless to be seated for long, positioned himself by a window, his expression having clouded over.

'I've studied the layout of the county seat, just like you asked me to. Also the court of justice and the special rooms.'

'Do you think you can make an entrance just ahead of me, and convince the judge and county attorney that you are acting for the defence?'

Brant mopped himself down with a soiled handkerchief. 'Well, I know how others would do it, and the promise of a thousand dollars reward will keep me feelin' courageous. Besides, you'll be there to prompt me, won't you?'

'I will, indeed,' Melindy promised, tossing her long brown tresses which she had just unpinned for greater comfort. 'You're goin' to play the part of your life tomorrow, Mr Clint, but you still have things to do before you can carry out the job to my satisfaction.'

Brant's back stiffened. He was showing signs of being a more formidable character than his appearance suggested. He did not think that he had missed out anything and his affronted countenance confirmed his findings. He pointed a handful of long thin fingers in the direction of his employer, who forestalled him.

'Oh, you're all right on detail, Clint. It isn't that. It's your appearance. You don't have the look of a first class attorney, newly in practice in Border Wells. You ought to look smoother, better turned out!'

The Frenchman chuckled audibly.

Brant flinched. 'It is all very well, but fine clothes cost a lot of money.'

Melindy reached inside her stocking top and withdrew a bundle of dollar bills. 'One hundred dollars, in advance. Buy yourself a complete outfit, as soon as you get back to town. Head to toe, you understand? No skimping, an' no spending the money on booze, before the event. That's my stipulation, an' you've got to agree to it.'

Brant nodded several times, his long fingers busy with the notes, as he counted without looking at them.

'All right, all right. I'll meet you at the building which stands alone, south-east of town. Around nine in the morning. At the place where you alight. All right?'

Having felt the money, Brant was anxious to depart again. Melindy rose to her feet in more leisurely fashion and headed him to the door.

'You wouldn't entertain ideas about double-crossin' us, would you, Clint?'

Instead of going hastily through the

door, Brant backed off, as if before a physical threat. After thrusting his wad of notes into an inner pocket, he waved his over-long arms about, looked for support from the Frenchman in vain, and finally groaned.

Melindy pointed her cigar at him. 'I get the impression you are easily put off, especially in a tight situation. Don't forget you're one of a team. I don't like bein' let down. I have been let down before, an' still I'm here. Recent setbacks have made me mean, Clint. So be careful. There was something else you were supposed to check out for me which we haven't mentioned.'

The shifty clerk stopped waving about. The thoughtful expression returned to his face.

'You mean about our common enemy, Mike Liddell?'

Melindy nodded, and Guerin showed a marked interest.

'He's nowhere in town, I promise you, miss. He's the only one who might have shaken me in my determination to make this caper work. A man to watch, at all times. But for some reason he's missin' from Sunrise at this vital time.'

'Let's hope it stays that way, Mr Brant. That way, nothing's goin' to put you off, eh?'

Swinging her hips in a provocative fashion, Melindy-Lou backed off and allowed the visitor to reach the outside. She watched him, sharing Guerin's window, until he had mounted up and ridden out of sight again.

The prisoner had been wondering why Melindy didn't take the chance to escape with him in the present situation, with two sympathetic guards at their beck and call: but he did not voice his doubts. He supposed that she had to do it the hard way, with drama, panache, style, or whatever.

And he was right.

9

On the way from the telegraph office to the more central shack with town marshal Van Walters' shingle outside, Mike Liddell found himself looking around to see if he was observed. When there was no one around, he dipped to his right hand holster for the .45 Colt that nestled there. Three, four, five times he drew the revolver, coming to the conclusion that the holster had stiffened a bit since he last had to use it for a purpose. That would have to be seen to.

As he stepped up onto the sidewalk which fronted the peace office, he found himself ducking this way and that, shadow-boxing like a fist fighter in training. Some time, quite soon he felt it in his bones that he would be in action. All these deep felt forebodings were going to rise to the surface. He knew of three and maybe more old time opponents who were in the district and up to no good. The prospect of action briefly exhilarated him, and then the close proximity of the peace office brought him back to earth.

He knocked on the door and stepped inside, at once removing his cream stetson and seeking to adjust his eyes to the shadowy interior.

Van Walters, seated at the back of his desk, looked up at him over his unprepossessing reading glasses, showed a marked lack of interest and returned to his perusal of a week-old newspaper.

'Good afternoon, marshal, I'll allow you have pressin' duties, but where I come from we still show courtesy to visitors.'

Constable Savage renewed his attack on a wall with a wet mop. Deputy Nevins came in just as Mike started to tap the front of the desk with his boot toe. The newcomer at once sensed the atmosphere. He had never seen Mike

Liddell in this positive, businesslike frame of mind.

'Howdy, Mike, something we can do for you?' Nevins asked.

'Sure, Rory. I'm here today as the accredited representative of *Madame la Baronne de Beauclerc*, of Sundown City. My instructions are to pay any fine due on behalf of one Paddy McAllen, collect him an' clear out of town for other parts. So, if you could tell me the amount which will clear him?'

Mike slipped the distinctive Beauclerc ring off the third finger of his left hand, handed it to the deputy and began to peel off his shirt. In spite of himself, the veteran marshal could not hide his curiosity. He watched the shirt being reversed, and the folded bills being removed from a pocket in the lining.

Nevins stood at a point between the marshal and his visitor, and looked down inquiringly at his superior. 'Well, marshal, you're the one to fix the fine.

How much is it?'

Van Walters looked down again, faked an outburst of coughing. Nevins shrugged, and Mike grinned. He remarked: 'Of course, it's entirely up to me whether I decide to pay for damage done to a door at the rear of the peace office. I make my own decisions in cases like these. One thing does put me off, though, an' that's bein' kept waitin' when my employer is ill.'

Grudgingly, the veteran marshal came to life. He sniffed. 'It was a good door. Took two men several hours to fix it back like it was new. Besides, this office ain't doin' too well in the eyes of the local bigwigs. They saw we don't do enough finin' of people. Get what I mean?'

Mike nodded and yawned. 'Name a figure, marshal, if you don't want your reputation to suffer any more.'

That did it. Up he came, out of his chair. 'Twenty-five dollars for the release of McAllen, provided you see he leaves town, pronto. An' twenty-five more for the carpentry out back. That suit you?'

Mike counted off five ten-dollar bills, pushed them in front of the marshal, who then glanced across at Nevins, who took the hint to take the keys and collect the prisoner. Mike waited for him to appear and then hovered about on the sidewalk until the last formalities had been completed.

McAllen came out into the sunlight, acting like a man with stiff joints. Van Walters called a query about the late McArthur's remains. He was informed that the undertaker had the weight, and that the older McArthur from Sundown was on his way in to deal with the rest.

Mike shuffled his feet restlessly. McAllen, on the other hand, showed no particular inclination to hurry away from the sidewalk.

'If I were you, I'd be ambitious to get clear of this town, an' that dingy lock-up, in particular. What are you waitin' for?'

'Jest lookin' you over, amigo,'

McAllen replied, mockingly. 'I like your ring, an' you certainly have style. How did you get the job of troubleshooter at the big French residence?'

Mike looked him over again. He figured McAllen for a man who did not recognise good fortune when it looked him in the face.

'It's a long story, an' time is precious right now. I have to get a move on.'

The troubleshooter quickened his step. Just once he looked back over his shoulder at Molly O'Callan's unusual cousin. Paddy was showing every sign of reluctance. He acted more like a gangling schoolboy than a widely travelled man of forty years. His shoulders were narrow. He had draped a buttonless vest over one of them, and his low brow was so furrowed that his forehead had almost disappeared under the shabby, dented black stetson. The brown eyes were close on either side of the sharp nose, and this homely defect was accentuated by the hat brim which was pointed at the front.

'If you're not up with me by the time I reach the livery, you're on your own!'

Paddy pretended not to have heard clearly. There was no attempt to repeat the ultimatum. The horse in the stable would have to be paid for in regard to its keep, and the Irishman had few enough dollars in his pocket to make that a major consideration.

Consequently, he speeded up and contrived to catch up with his benefactor just as Mike reached the big sliding door which gave access to the stalls. This time the Texan slowed down, and turned to face him. Maddeningly, the Irishman pulled out a plug of tobacco and started to nibble it.

A minute of silence built up between them. Paddy remarked: 'How a self-respectin' man could take orders from a high an' mighty French noble woman, an' a sharp-tongued Irish skivvy, I'll never know!'

Pushed too far, Mike stepped half a pace nearer and threw a right handed punch which landed on the angle of the other's jaw and dropped him in the dust, not too far from the nearest pile of horse droppings. McAllen let go of his vest, and retrieved his hat which had slipped off sideways. He rose on one knee, his small-featured stubbled face reflecting sudden hatred and the likelihood of consuming anger. With an effort, he kept his voice to a normal note.

Mike, who wished he had not let himself be provoked, was glad that there was no one near to observe the hostile exchanges.

'Now, I'll have to be wonderin' if your temper flared on account of *la Baronne* or her washerwoman,' he murmured temptingly.

Mike yawned, partly on account of the heat and partly to relieve the tension in himself. 'On account of both women, Irishman. In the west we always treat the women with a lot of respect. You'll have to learn to do that, if you want to stay out of trouble!'

Suddenly there was a blur of

movement. Supporting himself on his knee and left hand, McAllen made a grab for the right-handed revolver which had recently been returned to him. Instead of crouching, or seeking to put distance between himself and the Irishman, Mike danced forward, waiting until the big Colt had cleared leather. He then aimed an accurate kick at the wrist which made his troublesome charge drop it and yell out in pain.

'I can see now why you aren't popular with your own kind, McAllen. If you don't want to go on driftin' acknowledge that the Beauclerc money has been paid out on your account. Collect your cayuse an' behave yourself!'

Mike tapped on the dirty window of the livery office before pushing open the big door. McAllen saw to the saddling of his own horse and gave no more trouble. Five minutes later, they were clear of town and heading towards the east. Mike kept his chestnut on the move without actually driving it hard. McAllen's dun gelding kept up with a slightly greater effort.

The Irishman started to whistle, perhaps to indicate that he was no longer in a temper. The Irish jig did not do a lot for Mike's peace of mind. In fact, it only served to remind him how awkward some Irish folk could be. The sort of friends that made a man need no enemies.

'I'm glad we're headed west, I truly am! Michael? A good old Irish name, I'll be bound!'

The dun was still plodding along a couple of yards behind and Mike did nothing to make conversation easier. With an extra effort, the gelding came up alongside.

Mike sniffed, and massaged his face, forehead and neck with a new red bandanna. 'I'm not Irish. I come from England. An' furthermore, we're not headed for Sundown, so don't let me hear any blarney about the Beauclercs.'

'If I'm to be ridin' with you, surely I

have the right to know where we're headed?'

'You do, too. We're headed for the county seat. Due to arrive tomorrow. No time to call in at the chateau. For the present, act as though you were on the payroll, but on probation. Understand? You might have to use that six-gun to back me up before you are much older!'

Paddy whistled. 'Am I to believe that *Madame la Baronne de Beauclerc* isn't universally popular in the county, or is it yourself that has the enemies?'

The two horses manoeuvred together and then slipped apart again.

'Anyone who's worth a fortune in this man's country always has a few enemies, as I'm sure you know. I've clashed on several occasions with shifty Americans and Frenchmen on the make. Some of my enemies are massin' at the moment, an' I believe there could be trouble for us in the county seat tomorrow.'

Paddy prompted his informant and

was given the bald outline of what was expected to happen in Sunrise. He had heard rumours about an abortive kidnap attempt not long before he found his way into the county, but Mike's revelations brought it home to him that 'sitting on' money was not always an easy task.

'So I'm to take it that I might have to fire off my revolver against the enemies of Molly O'Callan an' her mistress as soon as tomorrow?'

'That's about the size of things, amigo,' Mike returned lightly. 'One thing bothers me about you. You haven't mentioned anything about the untimely death of your friend since I bailed you out. Anyone would think you didn't care for the Scotsman.'

'I did, I did, too!' Paddy protested. He was working himself up into a mild frenzy when Mike turned off the lightly marked trail on the north side, into a soft low-lying track which looked like a dried-out watercourse. 'He was foolish, but I couldn't stop him playin' at his

Highland game, the one called tossin' the caber! By the way, is this a short cut to Sunrise?'

'It is not. It leads to an old homestead, long since abandoned where you an' I can get better acquainted.'

Paddy relinquished the reins. He rubbed his hands. Although they had not been riding for more than an hour, he was anticipating an early halt, a good meal and a long restful evening beside a camp fire.

'We'll only be stoppin' over here for an hour or so. We have to ride several miles further if we stand a chance of gettin' to Sunrise in good time, tomorrow.'

The Irishman's spirits flagged again. Mike steered his thoughts back to the demise of Quentin McArthur. 'Are you sure you don't know *anybody* who might want to benefit by the death of the Scot?'

'No one at all, so help me, Mike. *Why* would anybody want to do it?

143

There was no price on his head, to my knowledge an' no one looked like offerin' a reward for stoppin' him from shatterin' a door . . . No, I'm baffled.'

'Did you meet anyone you would class as unusual in your recent travels?' Mike prompted.

The Irishman talked of Kauffman and Prusse at the end of wire, and then concentrated upon some of the more outstanding personalities handling the wire, the poles and the mules. The Texan listened attentively, but by the time they were crossing the swale to the abandoned cabin, he felt sure that he had not heard any mention of his known enemies, or Melindy-Lou's friends.

The cabin in question had not been regularly occupied for five years. It housed cobwebs, small running creatures, an elf owl and many kinds of insects. And yet the loft looked dry, and the roof appeared to be quite durable.

Mike made a lot of dust as he coaxed a fire in the pot-bellied stove, but the coffee was soon bubbling and McAllen was again revising his opinion of the man who had rescued him from the cell. Clearly, Liddell was no dude. He could fend for himself between towns.

The Irishman dawdled over his drink, enjoying the creakings of an ancient rocking chair. Mike, by contrast, went round the back and found a sack of empty bottles. These he ranged out along a low wall made out of dry stones. There were ten, in all.

Curiosity brought the Irishman out, and now he knew that they were about to do some shooting practice. At a reasonable distance, Paddy was invited to use his revolver. He blinked a couple of times, made a sudden and unnecessary draw, and blasted five bottles with his six shots.

While he was fumbling for more cartridges, Mike turned to face the building. He drew his Colt without making any fuss, swiftly turned to face the targets and picked off the other five, making short careful intervals between each aim.

'I'd like for you to practice some more,' Mike requested.

Paddy finished reloading and swallowed his disappointment over a contest which was about to be terminated right at the outset. This time he quelled his indignation, but was not in any hurry to recommence. Without satisfying his curiosity, Mike tended the horses, giving them a cursory grooming and then going off with his Winchester into a nearby copse.

As soon as he had gone, Paddy lost interest in his programme, but he fired off a few more rounds to give the impression he was busy. Meanwhile, in the distance, he heard two rifle shots and presently Mike came back with a jackrabbit slung over his shoulder. The Texan had a genial expression on his face as they met again.

'Sure you wouldn't like to make camp here?' Paddy queried.

'Nope. Like I said, we have ground to cover before we bed down. Wanted to ask you if you knew anyone with a name like Rufus Higgs. Does it ring a bell?'

As they tightened their saddle girths prior to starting out again, Mike watched his partner closely. A change came over the homely Irish face, and after a time, the close-set eyes brightened.

'Why sure, that rings a bell. Two fellows, drove a grocery wagon out to the end of wire. One called Rufe an' the other called Wally — like the name painted on the outfit.'

Mike described the pair of them, knowing full well from other times the appearance of Simmons and Higgs.

'It's a funny thing, you know,' Paddy remarked, scratching his head. 'After you got me sprung from the cell I never did get to see the wagon again.'

'The wagon an' the pardners sort of disappeared, Paddy. Which, as you reckon, is kind of funny. That pair of mean hombres have acted against the best interests of the Beauclerc outfit.

They could be among those you might have to use your gun against. *Comprende?*'

After a short pause, Paddy nodded. Before they rode on again, he had fished a second holster out of his saddle pocket and hung another six-gun on his belt.

10

At times the route towards the north-east was little more than an animal track. Sand drifted and made things uncomfortable for the riders as well as slowing down their rate of progress.

Around six in the evening, McAllen kept well up with his companion and shot him meaningful glances from time to time. Mike knew when the other's gaze was upon him, but he ignored the pressure being put upon him. Mostly he just sat out the staring. Occasionally, he unslung his saddle canteen and rinsed his mouth with lukewarm water.

Towards seven o'clock the terrain altered. The soil became firmer, more vegetation appeared. Sage brush clumps were occasionally punctuated by stunted oaks and pine trees. And the shadows changed. One thing a man on horseback, doing a punishing ride, could always take note of: his shifting shadow.

When they started out their shadows and those of their mounts were foreshortened. Gradually, they lengthened: altering shape from time to time as the stony track shifted its contours, but always hovering out in front of them, as though pointing the way and underlining the distance.

Shortly after seven p.m., the foliage changed once again. Bushes and scrub grew to a rough pattern as their little-used track converged with the wider trail linking the southern, railway town of South Sunset with the more centrally placed settlement, Sundown City.

On either side of the major track, the route had somehow sprouted the inevitable fringes of large and small boulders, which in those parts acted as nature's borders.

There was a slight incline as Paddy headed Mike up onto the larger track. There, the Irishman stopped, his mount and himself steaming with the heat engendered by protracted effort. Mike joined him, and crooked his right leg around his saddle horn. Methodically, they knocked the dust out of clothing which lacked moisture, and mopped themselves down where the perspiration dictated.

'Mr Liddell, I don't rightly think you've forgotten about a proposed night camp fire. All I would say is that the jackrabbit ain't likely to stay fresh indefinitely. Know what I mean?'

'Yer, I know what you mean, Paddy. I feel the heat an' the saddle leather just as much as you do. All I'm concerned about is the distance still to go. How are you at gettin' up early to ride?'

'Oh, not bad, amigo. Not bad at all. Early to bed an' early to rise, eh?'

Mike carefully removed his right leg and substituted the other. Meanwhile, Paddy scanned the undulating dusty trail with its souvenirs of men, wheels and animals in both directions, pulling a wry face when he could see no one.

'One other thing, Paddy,' Mike remarked quietly, as he prepared to move on, 'do you have a pricklin' at the neck?'

McAllen let out a belly laugh without giving the question much thought. 'Oh, shucks, yes. Only I thought it wasn't polite to talk about a sweat rash on so short an acquaintance. I'll have to get me a new bandanna, as soon as we come across some shops. Here we go!'

Mike let him get ahead on the east side of the wide trail, and covertly examined the nearest adequate cover, in case they were secretly observed but there were no obvious signs either of humans or animals.

About a half mile further on the intriguing sound of fresh water trickling drew them a little way to the north side of their intended route. Even the horses put a little more effort into their work as they reacted to the encouraging sounds.

The stream had no volume to speak of. It came from the heavy cluster of rocks at the foot of a bulky grey outcrop, worked its way across a slight gully in timeworn stone and fell rather sharply through a gap in a low ridge, coarsely overgrown with scrub and spiked bushes.

At the lower level, there was a pool no more than six or nine inches deep which fed a straggle of undergrowth like a low clump of jungle.

McAllen sighed. 'Well, how about that, amigo? Isn't it a sight for the sore eyes of a man who has been on the move for too long in the most tryin' conditions?'

'It looks promising,' Mike conceded.

The Texan's eyes were busy again, checking the lie of the land, and working out possibilities, from the point of view of safety.

'I'll cook the rabbit, if you like,' McAllen volunteered.

'If you like, Paddy. We'll make the fire up on that low plateau, above the ridge and under the outcrop. If you approve. I'll peg out the broncs on the higher ground an' get the kindlin' wood, if you'll skin the food.'

Side by side, they flung themselves down by the pool, slaking their thirst with slow deliberation. Next, it was the turn of the horses. The chestnut and the dun gelding muddied it a bit, but the steady flow from higher ground had cleared it again by the time Mike had stripped off the saddles and blankets and removed the steaming quadrupeds to the chosen spot.

There was stunted grass not far from the spot which the Texan had chosen for the camp fire. He led the horses to the patch, and rubbed them down lightly before busying himself with the collection of fire wood.

Soon, the flames were licking up and sparks flying. By the pool, Paddy whistled and occasionally sharpened his knife blade on the stone around the water's edge. They came together on the higher ground, where the animal was turned on a spit. Coffee boiled before the rabbit was ready, and a can of beans had been heated.

'Do we still have to rise with the sun?' Paddy asked, as he rubbed off the tin plates and replenished the coffee mugs.

Mike nodded. 'Tomorrow will be a critical day for Beauclerc affairs. We have to hit the county seat as early as possible, and we won't know the total outcome until several hours later. I'll tell you some of the detail in the morning.'

The Irishman dished out the beans as the light gradually faded in the west, and made a careful job of removing the meat from the skeleton of the rabbit. Their meal was finished in twilight, and the fire had to be replenished with wood to give them sufficient illumination to finish off.

As darkness closed in upon them, Mike produced a couple of stogies. Soon, the air was filled with the aroma of cigar smoke, and yet the young Texan was not as relaxed as his companion. Earlier, when he had asked if McAllen had a prickling at the neck, he had meant the sort of sensation caused by the knowledge that some hidden person had them under observation.

Was it that which prevented him from actually resting? In the open, a man had to learn to trust his instincts. But he could have been wrong. There were so many imponderable items in the doings of the Beauclerc family that an imminent clash, or troublesome explanations in the county seat, might be getting on his nerves.

McAllen spent a lot of time watching him, as he smoked. 'Why don't you turn in, even if you don't sleep? After all, you're the one carryin' the load of responsibility. If you like, I'll move down to pool level an' keep a sharp lookout. I won't fall asleep.'

Mike studied the other fellow, who was teasing bits of rabbit out of his teeth. His first reaction was to refuse the offer, but on reflection, he decided that he might learn a bit more about how reliable the Irishman was.

'All right, then, I accept your offer. Stay by the pool, an' keep your weapons to hand. If anyone creeps up on us, don't hesitate to use them. Honest folk don't creep up on a night camp. Neither Indians nor whites.'

Cluttered with his Henry rifle and his bedroll, Paddy stumbled off through the gap to the pool on the lower level. Clearly, Liddell was jumpy and time would tell if it was with good reason.

*　*　*

The two men who had dogged Liddell and McAllen from the Sundown City trail had used all the cunning they could muster to keep their movements quiet and their presence unnoticed. Revenge prolonged their patience long after it would have given out in ordinary circumstances.

About an hour after Liddell had made up his bedroll near the fire and McAllen had gone down to the poolside, the would-be ambushers crawled around the northern end of the low ridge and succeeded in getting past the Irishman's defensive position without attracting any attention.

From time to time, their empty stomachs produced troublesome pangs, and they had to remind themselves that in a short while they would be able to take over the camp site, the coffee pot and whatever was left from the other pair's victuals.

At first, the bulky man was ahead of his partner, but after a time he tired of crawling along on his stomach and permitted the more youthful, slim fellow to take over the lead. No sort of noises occurred to reveal the exact location of the Irishman.

The darkness troubled them as they moved beyond the flickering aura of light put out by the lowering fire. Fifty yards further on, they stood up, breathing heavily and wondering which was the best way to carry out their attack. The previous encounter with

Liddell prompted them not to under-estimate him.

Wally Higgs was the one to point up at the outcrop, which so closely over-looked the fire. Before Rufe Simmons could protest at the long climb to the top, in darkness, Higgs indicated the comparatively easy ascent from the north-east. Large boulders of secondary talus had fallen a decade or two earlier: far enough into the past for them to be rendered firm by stocky plants of a prickly variety which had held the fine soil in place.

'You want to shoot down on the fire from up there?' Simmons murmured, gently massaging his body which was sticky with perspiration.

'Think how it'll be! With the light from the fire, we'll be able to pick out the two sleepers real good,' Higgs argued, in a fierce whisper. 'We'll be able to shoot 'em to doll rags without any danger to ourselves.'

After snorting, and hesitating for a while, Simmons agreed. 'All right, all right. Lead the way, but mind you don't blunder into their mounts 'cause there's nothin' so restless as broncs, sleepin' in unfamiliar places.'

A minute or two later, the ascent began. The rocks of the talus were firmly in place, but awkward to climb over. Soon, they were breathless afresh and their shoulder weapons dragged like a crippled limb. Fully fifteen minutes elapsed before they had crawled to the overlooking rim of the outcrop.

In five minutes more, they had rested sufficiently for their reflexes and muscles to react normally. Simmons began to smile to himself. Below them was the fire. To one side was the jack-knifed shape of a sleeper. On the other, there was shadow beyond a rock, with only a hat and a saddle clearly in view. It was enough from their vantage point.

Simmons drew his younger partner towards him with a soundless, exaggerated gesture. 'I'll take the one where the blanket is clearly showin'. You aim for the other.'

As the bulky man spoke, a small rock moved under his hand. He clutched it, relieved that it had not fallen to the lower level. At once he had an idea.

He went on: 'I'll toss this rock into the fire, on account of your man ain't showin' too well. But be ready to fire when it lands, 'cause the shoulder gun ain't your best weapon. If they slip away, even wounded, we could be in for serious trouble.'

Higgs, the side arm expert, grunted grumbled and shifted a little further forward. He intimated that he was ready at any time. On one knee, Simmons half-hurled, half-steered the rock. His aim was good. It sailed into the dying fire, sending sparks and burning twigs in all directions. Before it had actually landed, he had resumed his prone position with his rifle to hand.

Two burning brands fell on Mike Liddell's blanket. He did not move, as he had previously crawled away, acting by instinct. A few seconds elapsed before the Texan came wide awake. The blast of shoulder weapons fired from a higher altitude spurred him into action.

While the bullets were screeching into the bedroll and the nearby ground, and probing the area where McAllen had left his saddle and hat, Mike moved up onto one knee and brought up his Winchester. He was working to offset the shock of the ambush, and also striving to think clearly about his partner.

As the flying lead came from above, this could scarcely be an act of treachery on McAllen's part, but he was at least guilty of botching the job of lookout. Almost simultaneously, the guns on the lower level went into action. McAllen, who was caught unawares, fired in and around the camp site, where he could take a sighting through the gap.

Mike, meanwhile, fired off six telling shots into the rimrock at a steep angle. On his third shot there was a cry, and the second of two rifles firing from above abruptly fell silent. All he could conclude was that one of their enemies had been winged by a ricochet.

Soon, McAllen was panning his rifle round and firing along the rim. One more shot from above probed his position beside the pool, and then Mike and he were firing alone. Each of them emptied a magazine and paused. The silence grew as the echoes faded.

'You all right, Mike?' McAllen's voice betrayed his concern.

'Yer, but no thanks to you, amigo!' Mike called back. 'If I'd been up there by the fire I'd be dead now.'

'What'll we do now?'

'You take the north side an' I'll go this way. Be careful. It's my belief they'll be scramblin' down the rear side, whoever they are!'

The minutes dragged as the pair threw themselves into the pursuit, where the blackness made everything neutral. McAllen moved cautiously to the gap in the ridge before he started to circle the north, and that particular move left useful space for the attackers to retreat along the same route by which they had approached without stumbling over him.

Shifting stones and the occasional crack of a dried twig under foot warned the searchers that they were closing on one another. When only the narrowing lower slope of the outcrop separated them, it became obvious that their attackers had somehow managed to get down to the lower level unnoticed.

By tacit consent, the troubled Irishman and the angry Texan paused to regain their breath and rest up.

Two or three minutes later, the muted sounds of saddle trappings and horses hooves confirmed that the ambushers had reached their mounts and achieved a healthy retreat.

Back at the camp, Mike's blanket and his partner's hat had bullet holes in them; signs which did not augur well for a new partnership involving firearms.

11

The new county town of Sunrise lived up to its name on the day when the judge of the county circuit, Thomas E. Blades, was due to try his first case in the county court-house at the rear of the dusty and as yet ill-defined square.

The judge, the officers of the court, the sheriff's department and that of the town marshal were all much in evidence within an hour of sunrise. The two eating houses were busy, and the newly opened-up hotel and rooming houses all showed their respect for the judge and the occasion by providing breakfast at an hour markedly earlier than usual.

Court officers patrolled the two-storey wood-and-brick building, paying attention to the judge's withdrawal room, and that other remote chamber at the rear, which was meant to house prisoners before they were called. Men saddled up their horses and rigs for no other reason than wanting to be seen around on this day of days, the official opening of the hall of justice; the spot where the judge was to officiate.

Over the previous few weeks countless rumours had spread all over the county about the titled lady who lived in the chateau north of Sundown, of the various fortune hunters who had molested her unsuccessfully in the past year or so, and of the impending trial of the rascally Frenchman who had attempted to spirit *Madame la Baronne* away to a faked-up non-existent family meeting in faraway New Orleans.

Everyone in the new county settlement knew that the chateau had been in a state of siege, and that a member of Guerin's gang, no longer alive, had thrown dynamite and made a general nuisance of himself, threatening lives and property over a considerable period before madame's personal troubleshooter, one Mike Liddell, had contrived to get the better of him, working against an ultimatum and a time limit.

Over the coffee, the gossip started all over again. Judge Thomas E. Blades, who had arrived from Texas less than twenty-four hours previously, was as keen to make a good start in the new settlement as anyone else. In his private chamber to the rear of the court-house he brooded over his last cup of coffee and permitted himself one small cigar. Blades was sixty years old, of average stature and an overwhelming personality. His fierceness showed in his piercing grey eyes, the jutting brows and the way in which he thrust his head forward when a topic of conversation interested him. His brush-like cranial hair was cropped short, grey and crisp. His mouth was a tight line, except when he was addressing court.

On this important morning, he had on a dark, tailored suit and a grey waistcoat, resplendent with a gold chain and hunter watch. His pince nez, on a black ribbon, nestled in the other waistcoat pocket.

The judge cleared his throat, examined his half-smoked cigar and blinked a few times. The man sitting across from him, Hector V. Sanger, formally of Nevada, speculated on what the judge was thinking.

'You think the troubleshooter fellow, an' the overdue lawyer for the defence will make it in time to start promptly, Thomas?'

Not many men had the audacity to call the judge by his Christian name. The county attorney, Sanger, was one of the privileged few.

Blades studied his questioner's appearance through smoke, as intently as if they were strangers. A slight pause embarrassed Sanger, whose full, creased face slowly freshened in hue. The attorney nervously smoothed down his black hair which had been carefully greased and parted down the middle. He began to wonder if Blades had actually heard him.

Blades chuckled, and then turned grim again. 'The authority of justice in the United States, the dignity of the law must always be upheld. I shall start on time, regardless. Any late-comers will have to give account of themselves. The warning notices about the advanced date of trial were all sent out in reasonable time.'

Sanger nodded solemnly, and patently wiped from his expression any doubts about the expediency of starting without a defence attorney and the principal witness for the prosecution.

At five minutes to nine o'clock, the judge started to check the time on the wall clock with that shown on his gold hunter. His tension communicated itself to Sanger, who cleared his throat, rose to his feet and opened the door a fraction. A fine clamour of voices from the court room itself filtered through to the privileged pair.

'All right, Hector, you go on in,' the judge advised. 'I'll follow you in a minute or two.'

Sanger nodded, smiled, raised his hand in a sign of farewell, and removed himself, quietly closing the door. A deputy guarding the door to the other private room indicated that the prisoner was already incarcerated there. The deputy shifted his feet and slipped the sling of his rifle from one shoulder to the other.

Sanger paused, drew himself into an erect position, and walked steadily towards an empty bench in the forefront of the court, conscious of the bulges in the knees of his striped trousers and the way in which his promising paunch heaved out over the top of his waist belt.

The place was crowded. He studied the faces, the atmosphere, the number of guards, and gradually forgot his own concern about putting on weight. The crowd became hushed. Sanger knew that he was the prologue to what was to follow. He wondered, would the trial become sensational, or would it simply be a case for the record?

The clerk stared up at the wall clock, wide of the narrow balcony. He exchanged eye glances with the county attorney, who nodded, and then banged his desk with a gavel. The murmuring ceased.

'Silence in court! Judge Thomas E. Blades!'

Promptly from the rear came the judge. The assembled were upstanding without the need to be told. Next came the prisoner, and there was a shuffling about on the plain bench seats, as the proceedings began.

Blades lowered his voice and talked to the elderly, stooping clerk, who intimated that there were no signs of *Madame la Baronne*'s troubleshooter. The name of the defence lawyer was passed to the judge on a piece of paper, but there was a shaking of the head in reply to another question.

Blades rose like a parson, nodded to his audience, smiled and resumed his bleak, business expression. 'You've all done well, gettin' here as you did, in

171

good time for this new county town's first case. Unfortunately, we are held up. I don't know why. We are informed that the plaintiff, *Madame la Baronne de Beauclerc*, is detained in her residence with a fever, but that does not excuse her representative, Michael Liddell, nor the defence lawyer, Clinton Brant who, I understand, is a new partner in a Border Wells law firm. It is a long time until I shall be this way again, so I'll ask the county attorney, Mr Hector Sanger, to outline the case against Captaine Charles Guerin, a visitor to this country.'

Blades indicated the prisoner, with a nod of his head, gestured towards Sanger, and settled back, as the latter rose to his feet with a sheaf of papers in his hand.

★   ★   ★

Meanwhile, outside the court entrance, a smart rig drawn by two grey horses, paused near the steps, while a lady

172

conferred with the man who had the reins. A guard hovered between good manners and watchfulness, while they talked.

Few would have recognised the lady in question as the ravishing brunette who had acted as nurse to the prisoner during his trip north to the county seat. Her slightly sallow skin had been powdered to a lighter colour. The striking hour glass figure was now encompassed in a smart pearl grey two-piece outfit with a spreading skirt and narrow waist. She wore long white gloves. There was no trace of the natural dark hair about her head and neck. Instead, beautiful blonde tresses were pinned back off her forehead and terminated at the nape of her neck in long, springy ringlets. A tiny matching grey bonnet topped everything and made her look even taller. Its short veil added a touch of mystery and partially concealed the powdered features.

The whispering concluded, the lady declined help from the guard and signalled for the reins to be handed over to two of the guards of the previous day, who were now coming up behind the rig and looking attentive. Hal Crowder quickly dismounted, handed over his mount to his kinsman, Silas Warden, and took control of the grey shaft horses. Clint Brant helped the lady to descend from the rig and at last the court-house guard was permitted to take a hand.

As soon as he heard the identities of the two new arrivals, he led the way indoors, signalled to the front of the court, where Sanger's raised eyebrows intimated a development of some importance.

The guard explained: '*Madame la Baronne de Beauclerc*, and Mr Clinton Brant, attorney for the defence, judge.'

Sanger inclined his head to the judge, terminated his remarks, and backed away until such time as the new arrivals should be seated and have made their peace with the judge.

'*Bonjour, Monsieur le Juge. Nous*

sommes en retard. Je vous demande pardon . . .

Polished French dripped from the carefully formed lips of the shapely blonde creature, whose interest flickered from the judge to the prosecuting attorney, and then to her escort the defence lawyer.

Blades cleared his throat. '*Bonjour, madame*. The court had not expected you on account of your illness. Nevertheless, you are welcome. Your escort, I presume, is the defence attorney from Border Wells. If only we had the other person here, your er . . . Mike Liddell!'

Melindy-Lou changed smoothly to English for her explanation.

'My fever is the cause of my lateness, judge. Unfortunately, I had to delay Mr Brant, the defence lawyer to assist me. May I, at the outset, have permission to address the court? You will know that my er, the Beauclerc affairs have not been running at all smoothly. There are things I can reveal which will most certainly save the wasting of the court's time.'

Blades liked always to conduct every detail of court procedure, but on this occasion the way in which *la Baronne* ogled him, and gestured to the visitors denied him the right to be brusque. He managed to fumble out the precious gold hunter and compare its reading with the wall clock before summoning up his best manners and giving over the floor to this splendid female plaintiff.

'Very well, madame. Would you care to sit?'

Melindy-Lou graciously lowered her head, but she declined to sit down. From a standing position wide of the bench where Clint Brant had subsided, she faced the benches.

'Citizens of the United States. Neighbours of Sunset County, I who was recently removed from my home on a pretext, nay, kidnapped, have not been as clear as I would have liked over those hectic days when my life was in danger and my property threatened.'

A murmur went through the listeners, while she turned her head with a slight show of reluctance in the direction of Charles Guerin. A smile flickered on and off her lips, and he appeared to respond a little.

'I have changed my opinion of the prisoner, Charles Guerin.'

There was momentary uproar, which faded again without any act on behalf of the judge, who was equally non-plussed.

She resumed. 'Since I have had time to mull over the attacks on my person and my property I have come to the conclusion that the true villain of the piece was none other than Wilbur Grunfeld, who died in the basement of my home when he was attempting to steal from the safe!'

There was another brief uproar. Blades and Sanger's eye glances were locked for a moment or two. They were even more surprised when Clint Brant rose to his feet and gestured with both hands to get silence.

'Grunfeld was shot by one of my servants. The other men, the ones who had most to do with my abduction, also died at the hands of those who sought to free me. Only the reckless, misguided Capitaine Guerin has survived, and he — by this time — no doubt realises that he was the dupe of Grunfeld, lured into acts which he would never have contemplated in ordinary circumstances.'

Guerin responded with a stiff military bow, from the waist. Blades of necessity banged with his gavel, and for once, he was not quite sure how to proceed. *La Baronne*, meanwhile, dabbed her cheeks with a small handkerchief and blinked her fetching brown eyes, so different in colour from the real *la Baronne*'s blue ones.

Urged by his employer, Brant half rose to his feet. Seemingly rendered weak by her own emotions, Melindy-Lou took her place on the bench.

The judge made a steeple of his fingers.

'*Madame la Baronne*, all this is distressing for you. I had hoped that your man, Liddell, would have been here to shoulder the responsibility of bearing witness on behalf of the er, yourself.'

Melindy-Lou gently kicked Brant, who shot to his feet and addressed himself to the judge.

'Your honour, could I explain on behalf of my client that Michael Liddell no longer has her confidence? Quite recently, she discovered indisputable evidence that he had broken the law in Little Springs, being involved in the theft of riding horses, and possibly in the murder of the horse minders who tended them.'

The ensuing vocal uproar had the judge on his feet, waving a fist and holding his gavel like a weapon. He banged once, and achieved the desired result. In answer to his glance of enquiry, Melindy-Lou nodded. He enquired if the witnesses were, by any chance, in town and whether they were of a truly reliable nature.

Brant replied positively to both questions, intimating that the two former peace officers were already in the building. Blades, whose interest in the Beauclerc affair had changed, wondered how he could best serve justice in these most unusual circumstances.

'Madame, am I to believe that the fellow, Liddell, is no longer in your employ?'

The woman replied gravely and quietly, saying that she had not seen him for days, and did not expect to see him again.

'In that case, *Madame la Baronne*, may I ask what are your wishes, in regard to the prisoner?'

The pseudo noblewoman inclined towards Brant, who received permission from the judge to rise and speak for her.

'Judge, Madame would like the charges of conspiracy and kidnap to be dropped. Furthermore, she intends to pay any expenses incurred by the court in these proceedings. If you can see your way to release Guerin into her custody, she will be extremely grateful. She feels he has already suffered enough, in his loss of face and honour.'

Having made his most significant court speech, Brant flopped down. Sanger answered a summons to speak with the judge in whispers, and the outcome was as Melindy-Lou had hoped.

'The case against Charles Guerin is withdrawn. He is released into the custody of the gracious lady who came here to speak up on his behalf. I hereby order the peace officers present to look further into the complaints against the missing man, Mike Liddell, and take note of any evidence which can be furnished this day.

'Court is recessed for one hour!'

The conspirators, Brant, Melindy-Lou and Crowder and Warden, who were seated near the front door of the court house, breathed deeply in relief.

The prisoner shared their triumph, which had to be restrained for a while longer.

Unlike them, Guerin was not haunted by the possible last minute arrival of the man whose character had so recently been taken apart.

12

Judge Thomas E. Blades had a reputation for expecting everyone to work to full capacity during the hours of ordinary court room procedure, and it came as no surprise to Sheriff Dan Moores, former Deputy Hal Crowder and Constable Silas Warden, when the judge's clerk sought them out, shortly after the recess had started, and asked for them to meet in the sheriff's office.

One other man was in the party invited to hear the evidence against the missing troubleshooter from the Chateau Beauclerc, and he was already sitting in the sheriff's office smoking a cheroot and awaiting any new developments.

This man from out of town was veteran Deputy Federal Marshal Jan Wilden, who had grown long in the tooth serving in many capacities as a peace officer for more than a score of years. In appearance, he almost always looked the same. Over his long sleek silver hair he usually wore a dented dusty black stetson, which in colour matched his shirt. A grey cloth vest provided a slight contrast, along with a white bandanna.

In spite of the twin holsters which carried his .44s, he could look quite genial when strolling about a Western town, but his slightly bowed legs hinted at the amount of time he spent in the saddle.

As soon as the party was assembled, Blades accepted the big swivel chair at the back of the central desk, as if it were his right. Sheriff Moores, a reasonably well educated man, moved to a smaller desk and drew a pen and paper towards him.

When the introductions had been made, Hal Crowder was invited to speak for himself and his kinsman, Warden.

'Gents, the fellow in question, Mike

Liddell, surprised both Silas, here, an' me. We were servin' the town of Little Springs as deputy and constable when it all happened.

'The agent for a big company which raised horses reported that some of their stock had been stolen, an' that two Mexican horse minders were missin' from their work, out of town, an' believed murdered.

'Anyways, we had no sooner settled down to the disturbin' news when into town came this here fellow, Mike Liddell.'

There was a snort, as Sheriff Moores blew noisily through his grey walrus moustache. 'Sure! I recollect hearin' about that! In fact, I was mighty displeased when the hombre in question contrived to make his escape from the peace office. This sure is a big county, an' a fellow wanted for questionin' often gives the county authority the slip. But you were sayin', Crowder . . . '

* * *

By a strange twist of fate, the character under discussion, Mike Liddell, was arriving in the new county seat at that very moment, accompanied by his unpredictable riding partner, Paddy McAllen.

All up and down the main street, men and women were talking in small groups. Judging by their faces they were bubbling with interest. Some even clustered on the steps of the county court, which seemed to suggest that the court was not in session.

The dun gelding and the big chestnut came to a halt of their own accord. Mike and Paddy glanced at each other and took time out to mop themselves down. The former studied every face in sight, hoping to see one which he knew well. Sadly, he decided that there were none of his friends from Sundown. Not that he had expected anyone.

'What'll we do now?' Paddy queried, staring about him.

All the way into town, he had kept quiet, probably on account of the way in which the two ambushers had crept past him and jumped them the night before.

Mike opened his mouth to say something, but he hesitated, because further up the street two men in broad-brimmed hats and baggy blue overalls were busily hammering on the platform of a newly erected hanging scaffold.

Clearly, Sunrise was in a hurry to get itself ship-shape as a fully working county seat of justice. Mike's mind flooded with speculation. Was it possible that Charles Guerin had been tried already, after so short a time, and without the benefit of his — Liddell's — testimony?

They waited for a break in the hammering, giving ground to a Mexican youth leading three riding horses by the reins. A stylish buckboard also went by before Mike swung out of leather and handed his reins to his partner.

'Take 'em to the nearest livery up the west end, an' ask the ostler to give 'em the treatment, Paddy.'

'Why up the west end?' Paddy wanted to know.

Mike shrugged and grinned. 'Oh, put it down to my superstitions. You'll know where to find me. Don't be long. I have a feelin' that Beauclerc affairs are not all straightened out yet.'

Paddy sniffed. He knocked the dust out of his dented black stetson, gave his rounded shoulders a jerk, into a more fitting position, and started off up the street. He was thinking that other races than the Irish were prone to superstitions.

Mike seemingly, already had his mind on other things. He crossed the street to the steps in front of the court house, blocked the way of a constable, who was taking his leave for liquid refreshment, and touched his hat.

'Pardon me, I've just reached town this instant. Could you tell me if the Beauclerc case is under way, yet? I

understand that Judge Blades is offici-
ating.'

The poker-faced constable backed off
a pace, looked him squarely in the eye,
and grudgingly furnished the required
information.

'You sure are late for the trial, young
man. It's over. Judge Blades has called
for a recess. Better come back in a half
hour, or so.'

Mike shook his head, and grinned.
He stepped out of the way, remarking
that Judge Blades appeared to be a
more speedy worker than his reputation
suggested. The constable brushed past
him, and he ran up the steps, trying to
peer through a window to see if there
was anyone indoors to whom he could
report. His interest only served to make
another official guard suspicious.

'Ain't you thirsty, or anything, young
fellow?' the guard remarked, hefting his
weighty shotgun under his right arm.

'Who isn't thirsty on a day like this?'
Mike returned, with a grin. 'I was
wondering if there was anyone in there

I could report to. My name is Mike Liddell. I'm from Sundown. Could you say if the judge, or the sheriff is still in the court?'

The guard crimsoned up, as if he could not believe his ears. He coughed, produced a handkerchief and cleared his throat into it. When Mike showed mild impatience, the guard shook his head and pointed up the street.

'Where are they, then?' Mike persisted urgently.

'The sheriff's office,' the guard got out, at last.

'Hold on, they're lookin' for you.'

Hovering uncertainly between his guardianship of the court room entrance and the need to escort this notorious newcomer to the sheriff's office, the guard allowed Mike to get away from him. A muted call after the troubleshooter did not trouble him at all. He merely called back that he would find the place, and stepped along more briskly.

As he approached the swinging

shingle, two men just emerging from the door adroitly stepped aside. Mike went through them. He knocked on the door, paused for a few seconds and stepped inside, doffing his hat and trying hard to accustom himself to the shadowy interior.

'Good day, gents, I had intended to be in town an hour or so earlier than this. It was a matter of distance, rather than idleness on my part.'

The judge, the sheriff and the deputy federal marshal all looked up in sudden interest, weighing up the newcomer and speculating as to what his business was likely to be. Before Mike could reveal his identity, the door opened again and in stepped Hal Crowder and his elderly kinsman, Silas Warden.

They spread out in such a way that the three men already seated were slightly startled. Crowder could not conceal a note of triumph from his voice, while the older man gave a gusty chuckle through tobacco-stained teeth.

'Judge, this here new arrival is none

other than Mike Liddell, the jasper we were jest talkin' about! I'd know him anywheres!'

Mike rounded on the tall redhead, in surprise, nervously massaging his shirt above the belt line. The older man showed him the muzzle of a long-barrelled revolver, while his close-set eyes adopted a mocking glint.

'So what?' Mike remarked. 'I *am* Mike Liddell, an' I'm in town to witness against one Charles Guerin, who instigated a kidnap against *Madame la Baronne de Beauclerc*! What's goin' on around here?'

For a few seconds, the tension mounted in the room. Mike knew that something had gone incredibly wrong. He recognised the two men who had followed him in. As a result, his stomach crawled with foreboding. He did not like the way in which the sheriff, the judge and the strange man with the star were regarding him. They acted as if he was the criminal in the latest kidnap incident, instead of the principal witness for the prosecution.

'You want I should disarm him, judge?' Crowder asked casually, reaching out a .44 revolver.

Sheriff Moores reached towards a hook on the wall, where his gun belt and weapon hung, but the silver-haired man with the white bandanna forestalled him.

'No, that won't be necessary, fellows. I guess we can cope.'

Mike glanced in his direction. He was surprised to see that the speaker had a revolver in each hand, resting on his knees.

'Kindly place your hardware on the sheriff's desk. *Then* we'll decide what's to be done next. How about it?'

Mike hesitated. The tension built up. Crowder and Warden reluctantly left the building. If anything, having clashed with Liddell before, they had a greater interest in his future than the others in the room. Mike sighed. Slowly, he unbuckled his gun belt and discarded it.

'My job as troubleshooter to *la Baronne* has put me in ridiculous situations from time to time, but this is the first time I've hit a town as chief witness in a prosecution, only to be arrested on contact.'

Having dropped the gun belt in front of the judge, he stepped back, straightened up and shared his attention between the three men.

Blades tapped on the desk with a paper knife. 'All the cash in the world doesn't necessarily protect a noble lady from a scheming villain such as we have here!'

'I resent that, judge!' Mike protested. 'I've laid my life on the line for *la Baronne* several times. Besides, you talk as if you've met the lady in question, an' that ain't possible.'

Wilden, Blades and Moores all three raised their eyebrows and looked very surprised.

'Jest about every man in town has rested his admirin' eyes on her this very mornin', Liddell, an' that seems to be

194

more than you have done!'

The faces of the other two confirmed Moores' remarks.

'That's not possible, gents. *Madame la Baronne* is ill, at home. She couldn't make the trip!' Mike insisted.

The trio of listeners allowed the silence to grow between them. Eventually, the sheriff rose to his feet and collected his keys. The judge and the federal officer silently approved his course of action, and the stunned troubleshooter was steered towards the cells.

13

The roomy sheriff's office had two cells facing into the part where most of the business was done. For a time, Mike could do nothing but pace up and down and think of the ghastly situation which his own and his mistress' enemies had placed him.

Judge Blades talked on with the federal deputy and the county sheriff for another quarter of an hour. All the time they were conversing Mike listened and took in the details.

Eventually, a messenger came from the court room and Blades made an effort to distract himself from the Beauclerc business and think about other cases of lesser seriousness which nevertheless required his full attention throughout the rest of the morning.

Around midday, the prisoner was offered some coffee, which he accepted with a good grace. His dilemma had temporarily removed his appetite and he felt he could not take any food. As he was too restless to sleep, he came up with an idea which he thought might do him some good in the near future.

Moores agreed for him to have a paper pad and a pencil, and also answered questions put to him from time to time. During the afternoon, the prisoner was still writing and the sheriff left him to it, guarded only by a constable.

Mike's notes dealt with a period a few weeks earlier when he had tangled with the gang brought into the county by Charles Guerin for the express purpose of abducting *Madame la Baronne de Beauclerc*. He wrote of his suspicions when he learned that the official escort was coming up from New Orleans to take Madame all the way back to the coast in order to meet a youthful female relation who was supposed to be honeymooning on a steamship voyage from France.

His first difficulties had occurred when he rode south to take an early look at the escort, and found them to be suspect in their intentions. An attempt had been made one night to eliminate him, and he had survived and managed to capture their horses. In returning the mounts to Little Springs, in the belief that they had been stolen, he had himself been accused of the theft and also there was a suspicion that he had murdered the minders of the riding horses.

In order to get himself out of jail, and return to his mistress before the shifty escort reached her, he agreed to a bribe put forward by Crowder and Warden. He had achieved his escape, but only because a young man sent along to collect his horse had been murdered in his place.

It was only by the worst possible luck that these two villains had shown up in the new county seat at such a critical time.

Fighting off a growing sleepiness, he

added all he could about the apparent intervention of someone masquerading as *la Baronne*, and also about a defence lawyer from Border Wells who was not well known in the district.

At last, he could think of nothing more to write. So, folding up his papers, he slipped them under the bench, stretched out and put his hat over his eyes. Sleep came.

★   ★   ★

All through that first day of court proceedings, men, women and vehicles came from all parts of the county. In Sunrise, it was almost like a rodeo festival or voting day. The streets were churned up with wheels and fouled with droppings. Soon, there were vehicles parked all the way down both sides of the main thoroughfare, and all the liveries had a surfeit of business.

One set of tracks came from the west. They were made by a heavy broad-wheeled hearse with glass windows on three sides of its upper structure, and a broad box with shiny lamps flanking it above the sober-looking trio of men seated behind the two pairs of matched bay horses in the shafts.

As the hearse moved in from the west end of town, a carousing visitor — already inebriated — roared with laughter, referred to the gibbet and pointed to the hearse. He likened the undertaker and his black-garbed men to the carrion scavengers which always appear after a death. It was as well that the trio did not want to draw attention to themselves, for they had successfully earned an illegal living by robbing banks and stages before quitting the owlhoot trail and accepting the semi obscurity of a legitimate occupation.

Earl Marden was the proprietor of the Sunset Undertaking Agency. For several years previously, he had called himself Earl Martin, on account of his real name appearing on several 'wanted' notices.

Earl was a tall muscular fellow, over

six feet in height and weighing a good thirteen stones. His sandy hair was cut short. At forty-three years of age silvery highlights shone in it and his sideburns were distinctly grey. He wore a sober black suit. His leathery face was cleanshaven. His black Quaker-style hat gave an indication of his profession.

Flanking him on either side were his two long-term henchmen and fellow outlaws, the Bayer brothers. The one known as Rusty was the older. He had fair, almost sandy hair and a back sliding nose which gave him a homely expression. Sam was the younger, in his thirty-fourth year. His hair was dark enough to be termed auburn, and his nose had been thickened and flattened in a fistic brawl, so that his expression seemed markedly different from that of his brother.

These two undertaker's men wore undented black hats. Their sideburns had been blackened with a sober black dye, perhaps to show their devotion to their first legitimate enterprise. By a strange coincidence, the trails of the Marden gang had crossed with that of Mike Liddell many months previously, with the result that the troubleshooter and the former outlaws were now indisputably allies, and the undertaking company had served the Beauclerc household in some matters which could scarcely have passed for upholding the law.

At the time when Mike started on his travels to look into the wild goings on of Quentin McArthur and Paddy McAllen, Earl and his boys were still at the chateau making good some damage to an underground garden entrance which had suffered during a siege of the house occupied by one of Guerin's gang, since deceased.

Now, they were on their way to the county seat with the sole objective of assisting Mike Liddell in his tricky assignment: even though they would run the risk of being observed by someone who knew them when they were still outlaws.

Consequently, they were watchful. The horses were tired and needed attention. Earl was thirsty and in a slight temper, and the nerves of his men were slightly on edge. After an interval of an hour or two, the woodworkers on the scaffold resumed their hammering just as the hearse went by. Earl tapped Sam's shoulder, and he checked the team of bays right under the imposing platform.

Easing back his Quaker hat, and dabbing his brow, Earl called out to one perspiring craftsman. 'Hey, mister, is there anyone scheduled for the first necktie party?'

The bearded workman eased back and put a water canteen to his lips. Having slaked his thirst he glanced down at Earl again.

'Judge Blades has jest finished his first day session over there.' He was pointing to the imposing court house with the Stars and Stripes flag wilting on the flagstaff. 'This far, it ain't certain, but it's likely the first man will be connected with that Beauclerc business. So you could pick up a little work soon. The jasper's in a cell at the sheriff's office.'

'That would be the Frenchman, I suppose?' Earl queried. 'The fellow who organised the lady's kidnap.'

The bearded man stroked his chin. 'Nope. I don't think you've got the facts straight, mister. The Frenchman went off with the lady, *la Baronne*, early in the day. It's the troubleshooter who's in the cell.' He grinned and massaged his own neck, under his beard. 'Too bad if he has to get his neck stretched, eh? They say he's kind of pretty.'

Earl half rose to his feet and sat down again with a bump which affected the other two. He murmured his thanks to his informant, nudged his partners in the ribs and suggested they looked for a parking spot at the east end of town. As the bays took up the strain again, and moved off, the former outlaw-chief spoke in a stage whisper.

'Boys, something's gone wrong. First

off, we thought Mike could be too late for the hearing. Now, we find he's in trouble, an' the real villain has gone with *la Baronne*. An' the three of us know that *la Baronne* has never left the chateau. So Mike is on the wrong end of a conspiracy of some sort. We're goin' to have to be real careful on this one.'

Five minutes later, they found a yellowing patch of grass wide of the east end of town big enough to take their bulky conveyance and also provide pegging out territory for the bays.

Another ten minutes of concerted effort had them on the right side of the immediate chores, and in a position to see to their own needs and seek information. In a nearby saloon they bought drinks for a small group of off duty county court guards, who were only too willing to recount the events of the day in return for free beer.

All the time the three newcomers were listening, they were watchful for familiar faces. As soon as a singer appeared to entertain the drinkers, the trio slipped away again. In the privacy of a steamy bath house they discussed what they had learned, and tried to formulate plans.

While they were still busy with their own worries, a man with silvery hair, a white bandanna and a black stetson poked his head into the bath house and called out for Hal Crowder. When he called a second time, Earl muffled his voice with a towel, and intimated that there was no one in the building called Hal. After a brief hesitation, the searcher acknowledged the reply and left the building.

All three wafted away the steam which had obscured their faces from the intruder. Earl whistled briefly, and his henchmen groaned.

'Know who that was, boys?' Earl remarked, with feeling.

'Jan Wilden, in the flesh,' Rusty said. 'He's made progress, too. He was jest a deputy sheriff when we clashed with him in Nevada. Now, he's a federal officer. I'd say his eyesight is as good as ever, too.'

'I wonder what he's doin' in town?' Sam mused, rubbing his flattened nose.

'Snoopin' around, lookin' for trouble, I guess,' Earl replied, from the depths of his towel. 'It don't have to be anythin' in particular. I suppose his presence gives a bit of prestige on the openin' day of a new county court-house. All the same, we have to assume his memory is as good as ever.'

As the steam dispersed, they dried and dressed themselves hastily. This far they had not been particularly hungry. Now, the reaction set in. The glimpse of a hostile face from their owlhooting days had put an edge on everything, and coming at a time when they might have to bend the law a little to free a friend it was an exceptionally sharp edge.

When they were fully dressed, and ready to step out into the street they perceived the proprietor of the bath house coming back from the saloon.

'What's our next move, Earl?' Sam murmured.

'Food, Sam. An eating house near the sheriff's office. Maybe we can contact Mike through food. What do you say?'

The brothers nodded together. Rusty put the money on a shelf and led the way out through the rear door, just as the owner came in. A pointing finger indicated the cash, and took away his only fear, that of missing a payment. So it was that the trio left the building without drawing attention to themselves.

Well up the street, they encountered a constable coming out of the sheriff's office and endeavoured to find out if the prisoner had been fed. Without suspecting their motives, the officer in question intimated that Liddell had shown little appetite this far.

Their nostrils were being teased by the savoury smells coming away from the cooking department of two conscientious Chinese from the west coast.

Earl ordered ham and two eggs and some fruit pie and coffee to go with it.

In the brief interval it took to prepare, he retired to a table in a quiet corner and wrote out a message on a sheet of white paper, the sort used by the management for table cloths.

'All right, who's goin' to take the food in?' Earl murmured.

Rusty said: 'I'll go take a look through the sheriff's window, in case Wilden is visitin' in there.'

Earl nodded his approval, and indicated that Sam might as well do the actual chore. Whistling to himself, Earl appropriated a tray, spread on it the paper, and accepted the food, each plateful neatly covered with an inverted soup plate. Rusty came back and intimated that Wilden was elsewhere.

Sam lifted the tray, letting his troubled gaze dwell on his friends' faces. The older of the two Chinamen, who had a wispy white beard, was distracted from conjecture over the prisoner's food when he saw the other two put a match to small cigars just a few minutes before their own meal was ready.

Sheriff Moores whipped off his reading glasses and fished in the pocket of his courduroy jacket for a tobacco sack, as Sam Bayer entered his office with the food tray. Sinking into his swivel, he glared rather fiercely at the newcomer.

'Now see here, stranger, ain't nothin' puts off a man with a queasy stomach more than bein' forced to eat food when he ain't feelin' hungry! Come to think of it, you're showin' a whole lot of interest in Mr Liddell. What's the connection?'

Sam grinned broadly, giving a clown-like look to his maltreated face. 'Ain't nothin' to do with me, sheriff. When I'd done wrong, my Ma used to cut down on my victuals. Seems some guy went into the Chinaman's place an' left a dollar to feed the prisoner. The China fellow ain't all that good on white American faces.'

All the time he had been explaining, Sam was crossing the floor. Moores did not seek to detain him, and only offered a cursory glance as the two-course meal with its enticing smells sailed across his work room. In the cell, Mike came to his feet, discarding his hat and doing all in his power to make it clear that his appetite had returned. He had recognised Sam at the first glance, and his spirits had taken a boost at this, the first friendly face.

Right out of the blue, Mike remembered that Paddy McAllen ought to be somewhere about, but this was no time to be thinking of Molly's shifty cousin. Murmuring thankfully about his returned appetite and the kindness of his unknown benefactor, Mike removed the plates and cutlery from the tray. He noted that Sam wanted him to have the paper, also. Acting on impulse, Mike received the paper in question and substituted for it the papers with his writings of earlier in the day.

'Thank you kindly, amigo,' Mike remarked warmly. 'It was good of you to leave your own meal and bring along mine. At a time like this, a man looks forward to a friendly gesture.'

Sam nodded, retired and chuckled. 'Hope there won't be too many drunks tonight, sheriff. It don't do to get new cells dirty at a time when the circuit judge is so busy.'

Moores gave him an oblique look as he left the office, but soon after the door had closed and Mike's eating made most of the indoor noise, the sheriff lost interest in the unexpected visitor and turned his attention to a newspaper.

In this way, Mike became aware that his allies were in town, and anxious to help, in spite of the presence of their old adversary, Jan Wilden. Almost as quickly, the trio in the eating house perused the prisoner's notes and put together all the disturbing incidents and happenings of the day, before they had reached town.

The notes left their minds in as full a state as the excellent food did their stomachs.

14

For over a quarter of an hour, Earl
Marden discussed the predicament of
Mike Liddell in all its known aspects.
Clearly, a big confidence trick had been
pulled in the new court house. And
only one person could have planned it
and seen to its execution. A woman.
None other than that same Melindy-
Lou who had already impersonated
Madame la Baronne quite successfully
on a train journey. Apparently, she had
the backing of a defence counsel,
probably one who had crossed paths
with Mike before. Also in on the act
were two of Mike's old adversaries from
Little Springs and possibly two of
Melindy-Lou's old sidekicks on the
train caper, Rufe Simmons and Wally
Higgs. Quite a formidable line-up for
one man to take on alone.

The note about the stranger, Paddy

McAllen, caused the trio to frown and argue. Where was he, if he was supposed to be backing up the troubleshooter? And was he to be trusted? Obviously, Mike had serious doubts about him.

'So we make a note of this Irish hombre, but we don't let him in on our plans,' Earl murmured, through cigar smoke.

'I heard a rumour that there was another condemned man about,' Sam remarked, although he was aware that his comment might be regarded as irrelevant.

No one asked a question, so he went on. 'A small Mexican, with a hangdog look, so they say. Got liquored up, over in Eastville, an' shot up a family on an isolated homestead. One witness survived, an' because a woman and a small girl died, he's very likely to swing.'

After a pause, Earl asked: 'Where is he now?'

Rusty, who was staring out of the window, chuckled. 'There's some sort of a bundle on two legs bein' taken along the sidewalk between two hombres wearin' badges right now.'

The interest of the other pair quickened. 'They must've kept him in the back room of the court-house so as not to attract attention,' Earl opined. 'I wonder if we can use him in any way?'

Sam sniffed. 'It's all down to us, then?' The other two nodded. 'Will it have to be tonight?'

'If we wait till tomorrow, a whole lot of hombres might get excited on account of the scaffold. An' Mike might get called back into court to be tried. If that happened, he'd be smothered in guards an' deputies again.'

'How'll we spring him?' Sam murmured, as they rose to their feet and prepared to quit the café.

'We use the hearse,' Earl decided calmly. 'We've got to think of a diversion, then spirit him away an' hide him. Once we have him away, he might have ideas of his own about future plans. So, let's take the air.'

Earl paid and they sauntered out, still smoking and hoping to blend into the strollers and casual sightseers without drawing any undue attention. They parted, and went in three separate directions. Their attention, like that of everyone else in the main street was engaged spasmodically by a single workman on the platform of the scaffold.

Ten minutes later, they came together again.

'It seems the peace officers' mounts have the run of a special patch of grass at the rear of the sheriff's office,' Rusty murmured.

Sam added: 'They've shoved the little Mex down the back corridor, probably because he's started singing a lament off-key, in his native Spanish.'

Earl examined his cigar butt. 'Me, I'm goin' up the scaffoldin' to assist that poor workman up there. Next, I'll come down to measure the little Mex for a box. Right? Rusty, you'll start things movin' by spookin' those horses you spoke about. Sam, here, can back me. We'll need tools, two distinct types.'

He laid emphasis on the word 'tools' and his two sidekicks knew exactly what he meant. He gave them five minutes to get back to their present position, and indicated that he would trigger everything off by whistling from the scaffold.

The Bayers filtered in among the strollers, and even though he had been in action many times, Earl's adrenalin started to flow.

* * *

The bearded fellow doing the woodworking on high had been abandoned by his partner, who had an outsize thirst and a basic streak of indolence. Jake, as the bearded one was called, was in a bad mood: low spirits had him in despair, until Earl's footsteps shook the ladder beneath him.

The tall ex-outlaw had slipped an apron over his jacket, concealing his offensive 'tools' which were strapped weightily about his waist.

'Let me give you a hand, amigo,' Earl suggested. 'Ain't but a couple of hours' daylight left, an' you sure do look lonely. If I get the trap to work, maybe you could help me out with a small chore connected with my trade!'

Jake willingly relinquished his struggle, accepted the stogie which Earl offered and proceeded to lay his soul bare about his own ham-fistedness and his extreme willingness to help a fellow tradesman who also had problems.

Earl peered around him from the high point. He could see the disposition of the L-shaped sheriff's office, the horse park at the rear and various other useful details in either direction. A huge plane was used to thin the width of the offending trapdoor, and five minutes later Earl had made the 'drop' quite efficient.

He started to whistle, high-pitched and slightly off-key. Jake started to show signs of returning interest. Earl lifted and slammed the trap a couple of times. He then slapped Jake on the back, knocked his big rounded hat further over his ears, and intimated what his own bit of private work was.

Jake grinned. 'You want to go into the peace office an' measure that little Mexican runt for a wooden waistcoat?'

'That's about the size of things, amigo.' All the time Earl was talking his eyes were busy. He had seen Rusty bending double and walking in a half circle around the cropping horses, and he knew the sensational flare-up was not far off. 'Let's go below, Jake. The air's great up here, but a man can get too much of it, especially when almost every other hombre in town is takin' his ease.'

Leaving Jake to carry the tools, Earl hurriedly descended to street level. Sam gave him the nod, and a fellow who was hanging about near the alley beside the peace office suddenly thought of something urgent to do and went off up the street. After checking that he was alone, Rusty put a light to the end of his gunpowder trail and stood calmly to one side, waiting for the horses to panic and make off. At the end of the park furthest from the office there was only a low, crude fence consisting of unsecured poles rigged across low posts.

The spluttering light went off without faltering. Some of the nearer mounts started to whinny. One of the more nervous lashed out with its hind shoes and that started the panic. Rusty prudently moved further away, pushing his frame against the building and just waiting long enough to make sure that the mounts took the desired route.

The snorting of startled quadrupeds built up. Away they went, causing more uproar.

In his office, Sheriff Moores, who had no other peace officers with him at that moment, suddenly came to his feet with a shout of alarm building up in his throat. He snatched open the street door, clutching his gun belt in one hand and his stetson in the other.

Jake and Earl, stepping forward side

by side, collided with him.

'What in tarnation are you two after?'

Moores slammed his hat on his head and fumbled with his belt.

Earl touched his hat and grinned. 'We were on our way to measure the dimensions of the little Mex. For a box, sheriff!'

Earl slapped Jake on the shoulder and leaned nearer the discomfited peace officer, who stepped back a pace, remembered the urgency of his immediate chore and thrust his way out, between them.

'Wait here! Under no circumstances go near the Mexican till I get back. Understand?'

The two visitors chorused their assent, and watched Moores hurry to the corner of the building and turn into the alley. The sounds of pounding hooves by then were beginning to fade. Jake hesitated, and Earl encountered a favourable signal from Sam, who was watching developments closely from the other sidewalk.

'Would you believe anyone was stealin' the peace officers' broncs from right behind the sheriff's office, Jake?' he remarked forcefully.

Jake, full of curiosity, took a big step in the direction of the alley. A couple of seconds later, Earl hit him hard at the back of the neck, and the bearded one promptly folded up and further reduced his consciousness by banging his head against the wall. Earl lowered him to the ground, and left him in a position which suggested he was sleeping off a load of liquor.

The office was unoccupied. Mike came to his feet and grinned a welcome. Earl stepped to one side, admitting Sam after him. Snorting slightly through his flattened nose, Bayer moved across to the key ring which hung in a prominent spot, and hurried over to the cell occupied by their friend.

Sam remarked: 'Earl was supposed to be here to measure a small Mex for a box. I figure we ought to do that first, amigo!'

In spite of the tension in him, Mike managed to chuckle. He was thinking of all the incidents and setbacks of the recent past, particularly that very day: and now he had a chance to regain his freedom, and possibly an opportunity to put a miscarriage of justice to rights.

Breathing heavily, Earl helped Mike to slip a rather greasy poncho over his head. He then encouraged him to conceal his features by donning a tall, soiled conical Mexican hat, alive with small dangling tassels.

'Amigo, if you'd ever been a real outlaw, I don't figure you'd have stayed out of jail for very long,' Marden grumbled. 'You need as many lives as a cat!'

'Where do we go from here, Earl? Out of town?' Mike queried uneasily.

'Not yet. Sam goes first. You follow him. To the hearse. All right? We hide you, an' if we're lucky we leave town when some of the hoo-ha has died down. That's our plan, even if it's risky. Let's go.'

Sam listened, opened the door and stepped outside. Head down, Mike followed him, clutching a few items of his own under the poncho. Earl emerged last of all, his right hand twitching at the prospect of having to use a firearm before going to earth.

No one queried his presence. Jake was still sleeping. Somewhere at the rear, Dan Moores' frantic shouts were drawing men out of their contented frame of mind and brightening them up to face an emergency.

A half hour elapsed before the town realised that the jail had lost a customer.

15

Within a mere few minutes all hell was let loose in the new county town which had a reputation to build and dignity to find. Sheriff Moores came sprinting back to his office to make sure that no further calamity had occurred there. Just as he sprang towards the door, the carpenter named Jake stirred on the sidewalk and rolled so that his trunk fouled the peace officer's speeding legs.

Moores fell down with a noisy crash which disturbed a whole lot of dust from the boards. 'Hell an' tarnation, amigo, what in hell are you doin' here? Up on the scaffold is your place of work, not blockin' the sidewalk!'

The sheriff groaned, checked that his jaw was working properly, and slowly rose to his feet. A growing feeling of foreboding was slowly gripping his stomach.

Jake suddenly improved and rose to his feet like a boxer trying to beat the knockout count. He grabbed Moores by the shoulder, and grinned in his face.

'Why, you know how it was, sheriff! The small Mexican, in need of a wooden box! My amigo an' me, we was intendin' to take the prisoner's measurements when you told us to stop right here, till you got back!'

Moores squirmed free and hurried into the office. He slowed as he perceived that the Liddell cell was unoccupied, and Jake collided with his back. The peace officer rounded on him.

'Where is your friend? The tall hombre with the short sandy hair an' the big nose?'

Jake fingered his smooth, lush beard and smiled, thinking to act indulgently with the sheriff. 'Why, we was hit from behind by someone comin' out of the office! You want to see the lump on my neck? You don't suppose my buddy would hang around here, after that? Shucks, sheriff, it's mighty painful! I'll mosey off right now, if you don't mind an' see if I can get a poultice on it, or somethin'!'

Moores hustled him out. After checking that Sonora, the Mexican, was still in custody, he stepped out of doors and clanged a triangle, which was a makeshift signal to draw his men to the office, only used in the event of an emergency. Sunrise was having its first.

Most of the guards and extra deputies who had been employed for the session in the court-house had already left for the great out-doors, in pursuit of their riding horses, without which many of them felt undressed and inept.

Gradually, the milling around resolved itself into those who had put their horses into stables on arrival, and others who had prudently found a special place away from the regular horse pound.

Years of bitter experience over much

territory had ensured that Jan Wilden, the federal deputy marshal, pegged out his black gelding in a place apart. For no special reason, other than knowing that mischief was afoot, the bandy-legged veteran officer skirted the milling spectators and located the gelding, patiently rigging it for riding and then pacing it round the perimeter of town.

By that time, the light was fading fast and the distracted peace officers who were still in town were walking about with burning brands, which fouled up the air and spread a sense of foreboding among all residents and visitors. After Wilden had been riding for about ten minutes, Moores — backed by a couple of constables — blundered across his path, his torch putting up a smoke screen. Wilden controlled the startled gelding with difficulty, and effectively blocked the path of the searchers.

'I guess you must be feelin' pretty annoyed, Dan,' the older man remarked. 'Sure is some sort of mischief afoot tonight, an' the Beauclerc troubleshooter has flown town, as likely as not.'

'Yer, yer, Jan,' Moores mumbled. 'I don't rightly know how I'm goin' to face the judge in the mornin'. I reckon someone or another will be demandin' my badge for this night's work. You got any ideas?'

'Play it off the cuff, amigo. Complete the circuit. If nothin' comes of it, take a posse out at the first opportunity. You could go without waitin' for dawn, if you felt like it. There's enough moon to light up all you need.'

'All right, Jan,' Moores remarked, 'thanks for those kind words. You want to come along with us right now?'

Jan Wilden nodded, chuckled, and privately felt pleased that he was not wearing the badge of the local sheriff. Within minutes, the circuit was completed, near the east end. Moores' hopes began to sink again, and while he was hovering about, trying to think of something positive to do, a series of sounds connected with horses and harness carried to them from an open spot, still further east. The sheriff allowed his flickering torch to go out. As soon as it did so, the four searchers sniffed the smoke of a camp fire being doused with water.

The deep-throated voice of a grumbling man touched off something half forgotten in the sheriff's memory. He started forward towards the scene of the campfire with his energies temporarily renewed. His constables took off after him, leaving the mounted federal man to bring up the rear.

Wilden called: 'Did you locate the coffin artist yet?'

Before Moores could reply the searchers were close enough to see the great bulky hearse, with its upper walls in stout glass, and the smart matching bay horses which were being manoeuvred into the shafts by two men, working in their shirt sleeves and wearing tall undented black hats.

A lamp that one of them was carrying

drew the attention of the newcomers towards the front end. Moores and his assistants moved forward to speak to the undertaker's helpers, receiving short brusque answers to his obvious queries.

Wilden, meanwhile, walked his horse to the rear end, and stared at the smart dark-polished coffin which was reflecting a little moonlight in the very centre of the glassed-in area.

Within a second or two, the fruity grumbling voice resumed at the rear of the vehicle and a man's heavy footfalls came round the tail of the hearse and came to a stop near the rider.

Earl Marden had an imposing bandage wrapped round his skull, mostly above the ears, but one or two loops had covered his right eye and he had to stoop more than usual to get a proper sighting of the man in the saddle.

'If you're thinkin' of pushin' some late business my way, amigo, forget it. I'm right out of patience, an' nothin' will stop me leavin' this town in the next few minutes!'

Sheriff Moores returned to the rear of the hearse and glanced keenly at the tall, stooping, bandaged man.

'All right, if you co-operate you might get to leave town without too much of a delay. So here's a question for you. What did you do with my prisoner, the one sacked by the Beauclerc woman?'

Marden gestured this way and that, showing a maximum of impatience and fiddling with the Quaker hat which would not go on his head on account of the bandaging. Eventually, in spite of the hour he managed to give out with a dry laugh.

'Well, I didn't murder him in order to drum up business, an' that's for sure. Whoever clobbered me over the head could tell you what you want to know! Rusty!'

* * *

Crouched in the lower half of the imposing death wagon, Mike Liddell was stretched out on his back, occasionally catching glimpses of the gentle moonlight, as one or other of the men prowling around outside cleared the pattern of holes down either side.

His spirits were at their lowest ebb. He really felt at that moment that his days of shooting trouble were over. Almost everyone connected with peace-keeping had him pegged as some sort of a villain and he was only on the outside of a prison cell at this moment because of the long chances being taken by staunch allies who had bucked the law for long periods earlier in their lives.

He blinked at the holes and slits and wondered if the time was near when he might have to use the small embrasures to fire outwards, as well as for ordinary breathing purposes.

In the few moments which he had shared in the company of Earl and the Bayers before he had taken to his place of concealment he had been told more details about Jan Wilden and his knowledge of Earl's former occupation. Now, Mike wondered if the bandage would serve as an adequate disguise from a veteran range detective with his senses fully on the alert.

Unhappily, he conjectured as to whether he was fated to end his days in this cramped hiding hole. The alternative was to bring his allies into further trouble which would almost certainly lead to their being apprehended for their earlier crimes.

He flinched as the rear door was opened and the empty coffin was moved carefully into a position where the searchers could look inside it. Someone commented on the quality of the lining, and Earl answered the speaker rather shortly as he was feigning a lot more impatience than he actually felt.

Eventually, Sheriff Moores gave the outfit the go ahead and the searchers withdrew, followed by the mounted federal officer.

The undertaker, his men and the hidden man waited for five minutes after the way was clear. Mike declined a smoke, in his narrow hiding place and wondered if all the perils of this latest clash with enemies of the Beauclercs were over, or whether he would have to hide and be hunted indefinitely.

The Texan would have been even more on edge, had he known how keen Sheriff Moores was to take out a posse and make a strike, in order to restore his fleeting prestige.

*   *   *

Paddy McAllen had been close enough to the sheriff's office at the time of Mike Liddell's withdrawal to notice one or two details about how the sheriff was drawn away from the building at the vital time, and also to see who was making the running to spring the prisoner.

This far, he had never set eyes on Earl Marden, or either of his sidekicks before entering this small upstart little county seat.

As he had mooched about in his spare time, since Mike Liddell's arrest, he had already seen where the hearse was located. Having tied in the tall man from the hanging scaffold with the unusual happenings connected with the spooked horses and the smuggling out of the pseudo Mexican, he had a good idea about the undertaker doing some sort of an undercover job, either for Liddell, or for the Beauclerc household, or — more than likely — for both.

Consequently, when the searching constables and the mounted deputies had run out of steam in the search for the missing prisoner, Paddy decided that perhaps he ought to remove his own and Liddell's mount from the livery. At first, he thought he might have some difficulty, but when he reached the roomy stable there was no one around to give orders, do jobs, or to restrain anyone intent upon taking out horses.

Ten minutes after reaching the stable,

he was walking Mike's chestnut and his own dun gelding away in an easterly direction. Already, the hearse had moved out. Fortunately for him, the wide indentations made by its heavy wheels had deeply scored the dust of the trail, and he was able to follow it by moonlight without straining his eyes unduly. He looped west when the 'sign' swung in that direction, and the going remained easy for over three miles. In fact, the snooper was beginning to droop in the saddle when a hostile voice startled him into full consciousness. He checked the gelding, and the chestnut moved up in the rear, tentatively pawing the ground.

'Hold it right there, mister!'

Blinking hard, McAllen checked the scene. The trees overhanging the trail-side rocks on either hand shimmered gently in the moonlight. A couple of glances were sufficient to show where the hearse had turned off trail and gone through the trees and a thick growth of brush which backed them.

Swallowing hard, Paddy answered. 'What is this? Some sort of hold up?'

'What's your business?'

'Name's McAllen. I entered town with a man named Liddell. I have his horse here. I'm lookin' for him.'

The low, fruity voice which answered him came from the tree screen on the north side. 'I believe every word you say, McAllen. Don't spoil things. Turn about an' go some place else. Right?'

Paddy worked his gelding into a slow turn, but stayed approximately where he was. 'I saw what happened at the sheriff's office. You can trust me. Liddell came lookin' for me over Pecos Town way!'

This time another voice answered, from the south side. 'Even so, take advice. Go back east. Forget what you saw, an' what you think you know!'

McAllen protested once more. A third voice suggested he might end up in the empty coffin. Three rifles clicked, and he took the advice.

16

Federal Deputy Marshal Jan Wilden cottoned onto Paddy McAllen almost as soon as the Irishman had emerged from the livery in town. Wilden had used all his trail craft to follow the Irishman without giving away his own position, and he was still far enough behind when Paddy received the challenge that his presence remained unnoticed.

Wilden quitted the trail until McAllen had retired, and then patiently followed on again when the four-horse wagon came back onto the trail and moved a piece further west.

★ ★ ★

Among the deputies and guards whose mounts had been frightened away, Hal Crowder and Silas Warden were among the first to recover their broncs. The reason for the shortness of their search was because the two animals were loosely linked together on a fairly short tether.

The use of this twinning rope had been worked by them on countless occasions when their activities clashed with lawful or unlawful groups between towns. On this occasion, Silas was the one to take the praise for having remembered the rope dodge, and it was only when Hal insisted on riding a fair distance towards the west that the older man regretted his earlier thoroughness.

Riding the trails unnecessarily at night was an activity which Warden had long abhorred. Along with his kinsman, he knew why they were headed west. It was on account of the Chateau Beauclerc being in that direction, and because the missing prisoner, Mike Liddell, was almost certain to head for the Beauclerc headquarters.

Silas started to voice his grumbles in no uncertain terms. He cursed Mike

Liddell rather pungently, and then turned his attention to the fellow who had fitted him out for the special dark jacket to be worn on escort duty.

'Will you shut up, Silas!' Crowder cut in bitterly. 'That fellow, Liddell, knows things about you an' me that could make us candidates for a necktie party. Besides, I have this feelin' that he's around some place!'

Warden was about to retort and explain the vastness of Sunset County when his partner started to chuckle. The older man stayed silent. Crowder hauled in his big dun and pointed off towards the south-west. All Warden could see was a low hogsback ridge, but there was smoke in the vicinity of it, and Hal was sniffing like he was smelling the remote homestead on which he was born.

Warden whined. 'If it's a false alarm, can we take a rest, Hal? After all, if Liddell gets clear away, we ain't in any immediate danger!'

Crowder raised his hand in a

threatening gesture. One behind the other, they cautiously moved off-trail into unbroken country, surmounting the near side of the ridge, beyond which some human group had a camp of sorts. Presently, they were nicely placed to look down on the camp and the hearse lay revealed below them, some thirty yards away from a fire.

* ★ ★

At that very same time, Sheriff Moores and a weary posse were returning to Sunrise feeling jaded, saddle sore and dispirited, after a five mile foray into the unbroken country east of town.

Much nearer to the hogsback, Federal Deputy Wilden was walking his black gelding nearer to the undertaker's camp. He had been forced to dismount about a mile back, due to the gelding picking up a pebble on a treacherous stony patch of track not far from the hogsback. Having removed the stone with his knife, he had refrained from mounting up again, in case the stone had caused any sort of sprain.

Perhaps three hundred yards on the north side of the east-west trail were two other men whose recent activities had not gone entirely as they would have hoped. Since their abortive attempt to eliminate Mike Liddell and Paddy McAllen from the top of an outcrop before the arrival of the latter pair in the county seat, Simmons and Higgs had not achieved very much.

Wally Higgs had a painful groove on the left side of his body, above his left buttock, due to the ricochet from the rimrock. At first, they had felt grateful to make it away from the night scene of the unsuccessful ambush.

Higgs' wound had delayed their attempt to get on to the county seat without loss of time. They had blundered about for a while before discovering a hermit-like old man in a remote dugout dwelling. He had allowed them to stay and rest, and the fact that he had on hand a gallon or two of first class moonshine whisky made them stay longer than they had intended. Higgs' wound which was painful when in the saddle served as an excuse for their indolence, although from time to time they tortured one another with impossible conjecture as to how Melindy-Lou had made out in court, and as to the possible fate of the Frenchman, Charles Guerin.

And, lastly, the devious one, Paddy McAllen, was still around. He had kept going in an easterly direction for what he considered was a mile distance. He had then dismounted, had a smoke, catnapped for a little over an hour and then resumed his journey on the back of Liddell's chestnut horse, in the original direction. Namely, to westward, heading for more trouble.

* * *

Mike Liddell was saying: 'I'll not stay by the fire, lads. The sheriff came near to discovering my hiding place back there on the edge of town, an' we can't be sure McAllen had cleared off. I'll get back to the old hideout to take my rest.'

The Texan warily stood up, hungrily munching the tail end of his victuals. Nevertheless, he was slow to move away from the comfort of the fire and friendly company.

'McAllen don't bother me, Mike. It's the likes of Jan Wilden we have to guard against. Or anyone who was wily enough to follow that lame-brain Irishman's trail. But we'll see. Guess we'll all have to sleep with one eye open, eh?' Earl winked, below his bandage.

Mike murmured something appropriate and slipped away from the useful ring of stone inside which the camp had been built. Instinct made him duck down and move towards the hearse almost on hands and knees. Having achieved it in deep shadow, he lay on the south side of it, away from the ridge and got a whiff of the woody smell which pervaded his hiding place under the glassed-in area.

He crawled underneath, spread his blanket and contented himself with staying in the shadows, between the wheels. After all, if there was an emergency, he could quickly reach up and slide his body through the downward-facing pair of trapdoors. He dozed, feeling far from safe.

★　★　★

Jan Wilden was aware of movement on top of the hogsback. He willed himself to be patient for a while longer, leaving his gelding near the east end of the ridge and crawling forward at the lower level with his redoubtable armoury of weapons and his spyglass.

At the same time, Hal Crowder began to have notions that he had spotted something important. He had seen the hearse when it was resting in town, and the more he stared at it the more he thought it was an ideal vehicle in which to hide a man on the run.

He said: 'Silas, how would it be if a cunnin' bunch of sidewinders hid a prisoner in a hearse and drove him out of town under the noses of a whole lot of snoopin' lawmen?'

Warden wanted to reply: *I'd say they was nuts*, but knowing that he had to fall in with his nephew's wishes he showed a polite interest. A moment later, Crowder had gone down on one knee and brought up his rifle. Warden, hunched in his own saddle and gripping the reins of the other horse, tensed up.

'What is it, Hal?'

'Oh nothin' really. Jest this feelin' I have, that someone is holed up not far away. I'm takin' a pot shot at that coffin.'

Warden had little time for his fellow men and in his life he had done quite a bit of back shooting, but on this occasion he felt himself wondering if his kinsman had had a touch of the sun.

Crowder squeezed, the rifle kicked against his shoulder. The bullet whined across the intervening space, penetrated

248

the glass of the hearse, carried on, straight through the coffin and came out the other side. Having fired one shot, he had to empty a whole magazine. Two bullets lodged in the timber of the coffin: another, fired lower, buried itself in the wooden wall of the hearse. The rest hit glass alone, and went on through.

'*What in tarnation* . . . ' Warden began.

'Take the horses an' ride on up the ridge. Make a bit of noise. An' keep your Henry at the ready!'

Crowder was pointing to where the camp fire was. Someone had hastily thrown water on it to give them more privacy. Warden did as he was told. His nephew was determined upon a strike against the campers and any slackness on his own part could plunge them into disaster.

'What's goin' on up there? Who's shootin'?' Earl Marden sounded angry.

Crowder chuckled, but did not reply. Down in the hollow, Mike Liddell had been within a foot or two of stopping lead with his body, but he too maintained silence, wondering who the attackers could be. While Mike lay prone with his Winchester to hand, Crowder began to make his way in a staggered run down the side of the hogsback in the direction of the camp.

Two rifles probed the spot from where the original shooting had begun. No reply. Echoes again. The remote spot was no longer a night retreat. Birds had moved on, the lesser animals had shifted away from the secret places disturbed by man.

'Ho, there! You men by the fire!'

Crowder's voice boomed out from a spot much lower down than before. There were startled gasps from the low rocks ringing the fire and a slight noise suggested that the defenders were shifting their position.

Crowder, from still closer, filled his lungs and delivered an order. 'I'm goin' to have to ask you to lay down your weapons, an' stand up, between me an' the fire! You understand?'

'In whose name?' came the croaked query, voiced by Rusty Bayer.

'In the name of Sheriff Moores, Sunset County!' Crowder added, 'an' I don't have the time to spell it out for you!'

From higher ground, and a different direction, the shriller voice of Silas Warden backed up that of Crowder. 'On a night like this it don't do to hold up the sheriff's appointed searchers, so hurry it up down there!'

Earl Marden again. 'What's the sheriff's special interest in us?'

The tension slackened a little as Crowder chuckled. 'He had his doubts about that coffin. Whether it was occupied or not!'

Distantly, under the hearse, Mike Liddell let out his breath in a long sigh. The evidence was slim, but he figured the jasper calling the odds had not traced them as a result of any special orders, on account of Moores having

251

already looked into the coffin, back in town.

Mike flexed his muscles. For too long in the previous few days he had been under tension. For far too long he had been aware of enemies, and now he was about to strike back. Even if it meant his taking to the owlhoot trail, he was not going to let his deliverers go under on his behalf. They didn't have to be taken in, or shot to death by any pair of hair-trigger gunmen taking advantage of such a night as this, when anarchy could so easily take over.

Almost certainly, Earl and the Bayers would have interpreted in the same way the explanation of the man on the lower ground. Morover, they were slowly complying with the instruction to discard their weapons and show themselves, empty-handed, in front of the fire. That could only mean one thing. They were relying upon him to turn the tables on the ambushers.

Mike shifted his elbows a fraction one way and an even smaller distance in another. He squinted along the barrel of the Winchester and wondered if he was about to gun down a man acting under proper instructions, and thereby put himself against the law, or not.

The man on horseback at the higher level, presented himself from the hearse viewpoint as a fine silhouette, even taking into account the distance and the feebleness of moonlight. The other intruder, at camp level, was almost in line with the horseman. There was a choice. The young Texan did not hesitate.

He lined up on the horseman, slowly and carefully squeezed the trigger, and waited. Almost acting without his knowledge, his arms made the adjustment for the second target. In the meantime, the riding man's trunk silhouetted in the saddle jerked and slid sideways. The horse leapt away, suddenly startled, spooking the led horse.

The closer target hesitated, his two hands held forward, supporting his shoulder weapon. Before he could spring about in the direction of the hearse, Mike fired again. The man who was his target appeared to suddenly leap forward and upwards, launching his weapon away from himself, barrel first. Crowder then stumbled on hands and knees, and he was still that way when Mike emerged and yelled in a loud voice.

'Don't blast him, Earl! He might have things he wants to tell us first!'

Two minutes later, Mike came upon the survivor of the two men he had just fired on. Crowder was standing defensively, his hands half raised, between the three men whom he had threatened so short a time ago.

The young Texan chuckled. 'Well, what do you know, the murderin' deputy from Little Springs! That probably means I've just shot his murderin' uncle, Silas Warden. What a small world it is, Hal! If only you'd taken my advice instead of hanging on, after you murdered that young fellow you took to be me!'

'Some folks never can take advice, Mike,' Earl remarked drily. 'I have to congratulate you on your marksmanship! We kind of owe you something on account of this trigger-happy jasper puttin' the bite on us. Come to think of it, you all but salivated him yourself! He's got blood tricklin' down his arm.'

'So long as it doesn't interfere with his writing hand,' Mike opined grimly, 'because he's going to write a full confession about what happened in Little Springs, as well as testifyin' to who really stole the pedigree horses. I reckon these pair must have been in court when I was made out to be a murderer. It had to be their testimony which turned everything in favour of Melindy-Lou acting as *Madame la Baronne*, an' Charles Guerin getting off with a clean sheet! I sure as hell would like to see this jasper hung as the first victim on Sunrise's new gallows. He deserves it!'

The atmosphere of menace was strong in the hollow. Crowder backed off and sat down on a hot stone. Although it pained him, he stayed down because his every move promoted a reaction in the four hostile men around him.

Presently, Rusty went off to take a close look at the man shot on the hogsback, while Sam roughly wrapped up the bullet graze on the forearm of the discomfited former deputy marshal.

Mike and Earl shook hands, chuckled, and then embraced each other. The soiled bandage on the older man's head was still provoking a certain amount of laughter, although it was scarcely needed as a disguise in the middle of the night.

A lamp was lighted. Mike, hatless, started to write out a long detailed description of the crimes of Crowder and Warden. Added to the obvious was another half page outlining how Melindy-Lou had masqueraded as *Madame la Baronne* in order to spirit away from the court a man guilty of kidnap and conspiracy to murder.

A good half hour had elapsed before the document was ready to be signed and witnessed. Warden's corpse had been brought to the lower ground where an empty bullet-ridden coffin appropriately awaited him. In the absence of ink, Crowder signed in pencil, hoping that his signature would fade or be found inadequate before the document was read by a judge or lawyer.

Everything went a little on the dead side when Crowder had signed. A brief, desultory conversation took place amid cigar smoke.

Earl Marden chuckled. 'One thing is for certain, as of now. Me an' my boys don't have to stand up an' swear we were at the Chateau Beauclerc shortly before the court case, an' that *Madame la Baronne* was still in her bed, there, never havin' left for the county seat!'

Within hearing distance, in a tiny cluster of rocks near the west end of the ridge, Federal Deputy Jan Wilden nodded grimly and permitted himself a wry smile. He had now guessed the identity of the man with the head bandage. It was clear to him why the undertaker wanted to look different. He did not want to be recognised on account of his owlhoot past.

Wilden was tired due to his protracted scouting through the night. Only will-power kept his eyelids open. He had heard a lot which clarified the remarkable events which had occurred recently in the county seat. He had to make a decision, shortly. The trouble-shooter, Mike Liddell was entitled to have his good name cleared of charges, but what of the Marden boys? Ought they to be taken into custody and tried for their crimes of the past, or should they be forgiven because they had turned themselves into relatively law-abiding citizens?

He leaned back against his small protective eyrie. A sharp rock as big as a man's fist dislodged itself and bounced, falling away down the rock-and-soil slope on the north side and creating more and more noise the further it went.

Once again, the nervous men in the vicinity of the hogsback were alerted. Earl and the two Bayers moved further away from the resuscitated fire into the shadow. Mike Liddell intimated at once that he intended to go off Indian fashion, along the valley floor to take a careful look-see around the end of the ridge, even if the rock fall was only some eagle clearing a space for a new arrival.

Jan Wilden remained spreadeagled, not moving, wondering if the small noise he had made would provoke more trouble from some quarter. To his straining ears came a laugh which sounded scarcely human. Another man; another person, no doubt, in contention.

Wall Higgs and Rufe Simmons, who had been alerted by the recent flurry of gunfire, came on foot. Having reached the hogsback, they rested in the long grass and dry fern of the lower level while they recovered.

Rufe remarked, as he corked the last bottle of moonshine, 'Will you believe me now, Wally, there's a single hombre hidden away in that cluster of rocks not further than I can throw a stone!'

Higgs made a round 'O' of his lips, and lowered the spyglass which he had used to confirm Simmons' findings with the naked eye. Fingering his buttock wound through his denims, Higgs agreed.

'Not only do I believe you, pardner, but he's wearin' a star on his flappin' vest. I wouldn't have picked it out, only he seems to be wearin' a white bandanna, a clean one.'

'Lemme see!' Simmons ordered, surrendering the bottle.

'We could take him out as easy as poppin' a squirrel,' Higgs opined. 'After that, we could see what it is below that he's been so keen to study. What do you say?'

Simmons chuckled. 'All right buddy boy, we'll do exactly as you say. Only, I need another shot of moonshine before we start. Any objections?'

Higgs shook his head, but while Simmons uncorked the bottle once again, the pale dark gunman put up his rifle and sighted on the crouching peace officer on high. Higgs licked his lips, squeezed the trigger and flinched as the recoil buffeted his shoulder.

There was a change at the other end. Wilden's hat lifted, spiralled and fell again, dropping out of sight. By the time it landed, the federal officer had lowered himself still more, cowering almost among the rocks.

Simmons sealed the bottle and grabbed Higgs' rifle. 'Did you get him?'

Higgs shrugged. A very slight movement magnified by the glass suggested that he had missed. Simmons called him all sorts of fool, and actually shook him.

'Hell an' tarnation, leave the difficult rifle jobs to me, why don't you? Keep him pinned down there till I get to the top! Then we'll see!'

Simmons screwed Higgs' collar till he almost choked. Then he pointed to the bottle, which he was leaving behind. 'You know how to do a cover job, amigo?'

Higgs coughed and nodded. Simmons squirmed off, using the ill-defined goat or bear track which had assisted their upward journey this far. Its curving, spiral ascent took him to a fine vantage point, where he could look down on the camp, as well as the badge wearer's eyrie.

Simmons blinked, mopped himself, and grinned down at the fire, the camp and the hearse. A shot from Higgs brought him up short.

'You there, yet, Rufe?'

Simmons erupted into his own brand of liquored laughter. 'Sure, Wally, I can see it all from here! You can move now, if you want to!'

Wilden heard the shouting. He knew without sticking up his head where the laughing assassin was located. The heavy whisper, however, which came up the fissure behind him, took him by surprise.

'Jan Wilden, from Sunrise. We met in the sheriff's office. I followed you out here, seekin' to know the truth. I've witnessed an' heard a lot, but two jaspers who seem to be liquored have me pinned down. Do Rufe an' Wally mean anything to you?'

Down the crack, Mike almost choked with surprise. 'Don't worry about their fate, Mr Wilden. Can you stick up your hat, or something?'

It was an old trick, but at that time of the morning, it was difficult to come up with anything original at short notice. Wilden hoisted the hat on his gun. So sure of himself was Simmons that he half rose before lining up on the hat and blasting it.

Scarcely a second after it had been shot away, Mike's Winchester accounted for the bulky liquored gunman. Simmons spun about on his two thick legs, let out a cry like an Indian at the point of death, and disappeared in a scarcely-glimpsed spectacular fashion, bouncing down in the direction of the fringe rocks and the camp.

'Higgs!' Mike called. 'It's your turn! You're wounded, I guess, an' you're takin' on several experts. You won't get within revolver distance!'

Higgs rose up and ran, risking the rocks underfoot, and leaping along with a six-gun in each hand. Rifle bullets from Wilden and Liddell hit him four times, causing him to thrash about like a frenzied puppet. He died falling, blasting a grey innocent sky with probing six-gun shells which finally went out in a series of fading echoes.

★   ★   ★

By the time Paddy McAllen arrived, towing the chestnut again, the camp fire breakfast was over. The federal deputy had his charges all lined up on horseback. Some were jack-knifed and discreetly covered. Hal Crowder was upright, with his ankles secured under his mount's belly and his wrists also secured, in spite of his wound.

Wilden patted the signed document, tucked into his vest, and delayed his departure for Sunrise long enough to hear about McAllen's plans. They gave him coffee and some food, and listened to Mike's advice.

'If you come to the chateau now, you won't be welcomed with open arms by Molly, or anyone else. You'll have to prove yourself first. This far you've been a flop. Go take a ride towards the Texas border. See if you can locate a woman called Melindy-Lou, who impersonated *la Baronne* in court. Bring her back, and that French villain, Guerin, who organised Madame's kidnap and a whole series of misfortunes.'

McAllen left shortly afterwards. There was no mention of Marden's former way of life, as Wilden went off with his string of led horses.

The party split up still further when Mike rode off on his chestnut horse towards the west and the chateau. His trail-weary friends were of the opinion that he would not adopt the owlhoot as a result of his recent gruelling experiences.

THE END